HOW TO SURVIVE GRADUATE SCHOOL

& Other Disasters

Stories by

MOLLY McCAFFREY

To David —
I am not going to tell
you going to hell! I'll
say thank you for inviting me
to read at Third Tuesdy.
Molly McCaffrey 2-21-12

MINT HILL BOOKS
MAIN STREET RAG PUBLISHING
CHARLOTTE, NORTH CAROLINA

Cover Photograph by Classic Stock, 2011.

Author Photograph by Victoria Taylor.

Acknowledgements:

Quirk: "Sliders"
Silent Embrace: Perspectives on Birth and Adoption (Catalyst Book
    Press, 2010): "Pictures of the Day I Was Born"
The Vestal Review: "Look Away"
XX Eccentric: Stories about the Eccentricities of Women (Main
    Street Rag Publishing, 2009): "The Other Man"

Library of Congress Control Number: 2011923702

ISBN 13: 978-1-59948-295-8

Produced in the United States of America

Mint Hill Books
Main Street Rag Publishing Company
PO Box 690100
Charlotte, NC 28227
WWW.MAINSTREETRAG.COM

For Dave,
who has rescued me from numerous disasters

Contents

How to Survive Your Last Year of Graduate School

[Poetry] is the way of making one's experience,
almost wholly inexplicable, acceptable.

—WALLACE STEVENS

Start the year fresh.

You've just concluded a leisurely summer of working happily on your dissertation and spending relaxing weekends at your parents' lake house. This is what life is all about, you tell yourself. This is what you've always wanted . . . to finally focus on your writing!

But it's clear that things are suddenly different. Your dissertation fellowship is not renewed—probably because you told the head of the committee that the idea of requiring fellows to do a presentation on their work every month was complete bullshit.

But that's okay.

You stand by your words and prepare to teach for the first

time in fifteen months. You decide to teach a new lit course, not because you don't *want* to teach creative writing, but because you think it would be good to add another line to your C.V. You're given your class assignment two weeks before the term begins, order the books a week later, and don't finish putting the syllabus together until three in the morning the night before classes start, adding a little bit of Tupac to the poetry unit just to piss off the powers-that-be.

Because you're still technically only a graduate student even though you're A.B.D.—All But Dissertation or Deceased, whichever comes first—you get the eight o'clock class that meets three times a week, but you tell yourself that's okay too because you'll be able to hit the gym afterwards and make it home by noon with plenty of time left to work on the dissertation. That is, right after you finish the prospectus you were supposed to have completed before you sat for your comprehensive exams ten months ago.

The prospectus should be easy. After all, it's not like you're writing a *real* dissertation. For God's sake, this is just a *creative* dissertation. And besides, it's all about you and what you're writing, and, like most people, you love talking about you.

But instead of being easy, you find it's very difficult because you and what you're writing about isn't really as interesting as you once thought—in fact, you're not even sure why you're writing what you're writing, much less if there are any themes or ideas around which you can unite the collection—so you crib as much as you can from the prospecti of those who came before you and hope you've created a document no one will care much about, especially since it's not one you care about at all.

This turns out to be an epic waste of time because when you finally turn in a first draft a month later and meet with your dissertation director, he—because they are always a "he"—says it needs to be a document that animates your committee and that you shouldn't have looked at any one else's because no one has ever done it right before. You laugh—because what choice do you have?—and ask in your most scholarly voice what you should do to fix it. Your dissertation director tells you to scrap the whole thing and start again. In as oblique a way as possible, he instructs you to talk about why you're writing what you are writing and who has influenced you.

So you start with who has influenced you and go from there.

There must be some reason you like the writers you do. But despite the fact that you've been talking about this issue for the last six years (two while doing the Master's degree and four so far in the doctoral program), you've never *really* thought about this before—you just like what you like, and you can't explain why. Much like your students.

And, besides, you thought you were supposed to leave the explaining to the people who are writing real dissertations. Jesus, you're a writer, not a scholar. But you force yourself to think as hard as you can and stare at your blank computer screen hoping the words will come. All that materializes is a paltry list of the writers you really, really, really, really, really like, and this causes you to think about how sad it is that there are only four people in the whole world whom you truly admire.

In order to motivate yourself, you make a pact with your BFF. She's writing a real dissertation, and she's struggling too, so you both agree to write ten pages a week. Or forty pages a month. Whatever. It really doesn't matter how you do the forty pages as long as you do it. That's more than a page a day and you've never been good at writing on a schedule, but you agree to it anyway.

The punishments for not keeping up with the schedule are real: no email, no internet, no television, no movies. And that's if you don't get your pages done each week. If you haven't written forty pages at the end of the month, it's even worse: you must agree to a punishment of your friend's choice. You choose online dating for your friend since she hasn't had sex in eleven months, and she chooses therapy for you since you haven't been on a plane in nine years. You absolutely hate therapy so you find this really motivating, and you and your friend meet at coffeehouses and libraries so you can work together and stay focused.

Somehow this works.

You write a few pages every time you see her and a page here and there when you don't. You finish a new draft of your prospectus—with which your dissertation director is impressed—and feel unstoppable. You're like Milkman at the end of *Solomon*: you're finally going to make that leap, you're finally ready to get back to the real work of writing the dissertation itself. First you have to help your friend write her online profile for Match.com—she didn't make her pages—and meet with your dissertation director, but then you'll be set.

Your dissertation director is happy or at least less unhappy than he was a month ago. But he still thinks the prospectus needs major work. MAJOR work. He scribbles lengthy notes on your manuscript that you can't read, and you schedule another appointment with him to decipher his comments. He is helpful, but you forget about the prospectus while you catch up on your grading, and when you go back to it a week later, you can't read your notes on his comments. You decide to give it your best shot because you can't exactly go back to him again, can you? You recruit your husband—who's working on his own dissertation and smartly ignoring his prospectus—to help you decode. Between the two of you, you figure out about seventy-five percent of what needs to be done and submit the revised prospectus to your dissertation director again.

This process repeats itself six more times, and by Christmas your dissertation director is happy—for real this time—and your prospectus is finished. Never mind the fact that you've spent half the school year writing the ten-page document that is supposed to outline what your 200-page dissertation is about. Just focus on the fact that it's finished and you can feel good about that and move forward. Spend a little time indulging yourself—fantasize about the no-holds-barred, Bangkok-themed graduation party you've been planning since you started your graduate studies six and a half long years ago. Do this whenever you have a moment of downtime for the next few weeks so that when you see your parents over the holidays and they ask how your dissertation is going, you are prepared to distract them with the intricate plans for this once-in-a-lifetime bacchanal.

In the meantime, finish grading your students' papers, so

you can get back to the writing you were meant to do. Turn in their grades early—for the first time ever!—and don't for one moment feel guilty about the person you failed because she stopped coming to class after Thanksgiving. Instead remind yourself how lucky she is to go to college at a time when there's no such thing as a real F anymore. Instead of an F, give her an NP—Not Passing—and be glad that, unlike you, she can replace that grade with a passing one whenever she wants, not like the F you still have on your transcript from the fundamental color class you took your freshman year in college, back when you still wanted to be a painter. And whatever you do, do NOT think about the fact that being a writer isn't really any more practical than being a painter and definitely do NOT spend any time reliving your only campus interview last year when the search committee chair asked you about that F, and all you could think to say was that your Birkenstock-wearing T.A. didn't like you because you wore Greek letters to class once. Remind yourself that was a long time ago and add, "Don't wear Greek letters to class" to the list of things you tell your students the first day of each term.

Even though you're not supposed to, you start thinking about that F and that interview and the fact that you don't yet have *any* interviews lined up this year. This is especially frustrating since you spent the fall term sending out over three hundred application letters and nearly as many dossiers just to get some crappy instructorship without the possibility of tenure at a "teaching" school—which just means you get paid less and have to teach more—in the middle of some corn field in Idaho. Not that there's anything wrong with Idaho. You used to date a guy from Idaho, and he was nice.

But, wait, where were you? Oh, yes, you were thinking about last year's interview. Oh, yeah, *that* interview. That job *did* have the possibility of tenure, but there was four feet of snow on the ground and the students were all holy rollers. The interview just happened to fall the day before Ash Wednesday, and they were all planning to see *The Passion of the Christ* at seven o'clock the next morning. And you had to teach Wallace Stevens' "Thirteen Ways of Looking at a Blackbird," which even the most cocky professor in your department admits is a hard poem to teach. And, besides, you're a fiction writer, not a poet. And even though your C.V. says your main area of study is contemporary American literature, it's really contemporary American *fiction*.

And so there you are, in Nampa, Idaho, teaching the overrated Stevens' poem and talking about perspective and ontology, and the students are looking at you like you are from another planet. You spy a Bible on top of one of their backpacks, and you feel like you *are* from another planet. The entire English department is there too, and you wonder what they must be thinking and why the hell they thought you could do this. One of them—who you find out later isn't even from the English department but from Art History and only sitting on the search committee to provide an outsider's perspective—tilts her head at you and squints as if she is trying to decode you the same way you try to decode your dissertation director's handwriting. For just the briefest minute, you think about why you're doing this, about the fact that you don't have to be there, that it's a choice to be there, and you actually consider standing up and leaving. Just walking out. But, of course, you don't do that. Nevertheless, you decide the job isn't for you. Somehow it just doesn't feel quite right, and you go back home and sabotage your chances by not sending a thank you note to the school in Idaho. It works: you are rejected, and the director of graduate studies says they will consider you for just one more year of funding. You get another campus interview but turn it down without telling anyone, lest they make you graduate before you are ready.

Now that you've gotten that off your chest, it's time to get to work. You have one week before you and your husband drive Bukowski—your ugly, worn-out Ford Taurus—to your parents' retirement home in Florida for Christmas, and you are determined to make real in-roads on your dissertation before then. And oddly enough, you do get some work done. You are working at a more frantic pace than you were last summer—when you wrote a beautiful, sprawling ninety-page coming-of-age novella and about forty pages on six (yes, six!) unfinishable short stories—because you have a deadline. You're supposed to turn in your dissertation before you leave for the holidays. You know that won't happen, but you figure if you can have it to your director in early January, he'll forget about that December deadline. So you write and write and write and write and write and write. And you watch movies in the evenings with your husband. It's nice, and if it were warmer, it would almost feel like summer again—just the sound of your fingers on the keyboard and the unspoken promise of artistic fulfillment.

On the third day of this perfect week, you really hit your

stride and are still writing at one o'clock in the morning when the phone rings. It's your BFF's ex-boyfriend. He's a second-year in your program, and you set them up to disastrous effect the previous year. They fell madly in love in about eight minutes and then spent the next three months realizing they completely loathe each other. You learned during that time that the ex-boyfriend is not only humorless but also a certifiable lunatic and your friend should have had you shot for introducing her to him. But instead, she forgives you, and you mine her experiences with him for laughs when you take breaks from grading papers and pretending to work on your dissertation.

Still, the happy memories of making fun of him escape you completely when he tells you that night he's going to kill himself.

It's not the first time he's threatened to do it, but it's the first time since you've known him, and you're not sure how to react. On the one hand, you know he's bluffing. He's just that kind of academic—dramatic, desperate to be the center of attention, and totally full of shit. You've known the type for years.

On the other hand, what if he's for real?

And before you can tell him what an idiot he is, you think back to your first year in the doctoral program—the year your officemate took so many pills that he never woke up, the year you went to his funeral and wondered why you never got around to making time to have lunch with him and whether or not he would still be alive if you did.

So rather than tell your BFF's ex he's an idiot, you ask him what's wrong, and you spend the next three hours on the phone listening to him drone on and on about his failed career aspirations. By the time you have convinced him not to Plath himself, it's well after five in the morning.

The rest of the week is a bit of a disaster—you never recover from that late-night call, physically or emotionally—and before you know it, it's time to hit the road for old people land: Florida.

The trip south is a thing of beauty. You have two weeks with nothing to do but write, write, and write some more, and sometimes you even hit the ocean in the afternoons for a swim. On top of that, your parents pay for your groceries and even take you and your husband out a couple of times: dinner, movie, the works. It feels a wee bit like they're courting you, but you do your best to overlook the awkwardness of having your parents pay your way when you're well into your thirties and just enjoy the experience for what it is: a festival of free. Free meals, free place to stay, free entertainment, free time to write. And by the time the two of you are packing Bukowski for the trip home, you've all but finished a complete draft of your dissertation.

But on the way home, Bukowski does what he does best: he dies a little bit more, and you have to stop in Cordele, Georgia to have him fixed. All the money you saved in Florida is gone before you hit Atlanta, and you wonder at the unfairness of it all.

But don't dwell on how much you've been cheated by life. Instead, go home and turn in the draft of your dissertation, being sure to submit it before the end of the first week of

January, so you can see your dissertation director as soon as possible and so he doesn't remember the December deadline you failed to meet. And refuse to be frustrated or frightened when your dissertation director—who only has office hours from eleven to one on Wednesdays—doesn't make time to see you until three weeks later even though graduation is just four months away.

When you finally get to see him at the end of the month, he has some constructive feedback on your stories, but most of all he wants to talk about the prospectus. It's still not right, he feels, and he asks you to delve deeper, to investigate your work from a more theoretical perspective, to think about the postmodern intertextuality at play. You remind him that you have never taken a theory course, that it's not required for creative writers, and he says he'll need everything back by the first of February if there is any hope of you defending your dissertation in the spring.

You do what anyone would do.

You panic.

And after you panic, you clean. Because cleaning is so much easier and more constructive than panicking. And then you look up movie times even though there is no time to see movies or do anything else for that matter. And then finally, once you've wasted enough time that you're starting to panic even more, you start revising.

You revise one story, revise it again, and then do it a third time. And then you open the next one. And you go through the stories—one at a time—for the next five days like you're Anne Lamott's little brother writing his report on birds the night before it's due. When you make this connection, you think of how Anne Lamott always seems so calm and normal and practical, so down-to-earth, how you wish you could be more like her, and then you think about the fact that her father was a writer and you want to kick her skinny ass because, just like everyone else, she has some kind of in that you don't. But then you feel bad because she always seems like such a nice person, a supportive person, when you read her work, and you take it back, sure that the gods of karma will strike you down for cursing one of the patron saints of writing.

The days go by almost as quickly as they did for Kerouac, and you manage, somehow, to finish a decent second draft of the dissertation and a boffo thirteenth draft of the prospectus, dropping off both in your dissertation director's mailbox before your eight o'clock on the first day of February. After that, you walk as slowly as possible to the classroom where you teach, and spend those measly five minutes planning the entire class period, a trick you learned from your composition pedagogy professor the first year of grad school. The students are half asleep, and they could care less that you put them in groups and have them discuss the reading on their own, which is the other thing your pedagogy professor taught you to do when you're not prepared. And while the students are in groups, you wonder if this has been your problem all along— you spend too much time preparing to teach and too little time writing. No one else preps for class, why should you? But after you send the students home, you feel like a turd. They spent thirty minutes talking about how horny Mayella seemed and how impressed they were with Atticus' famous one shot, making you worry yet again about the future of humanity.

So you go home and start preparing for the next class—preparing for real, not just half-assing it like everyone else does, and before you know it, you've cracked the teaching code: you finally understand how to get students to truly engage with literature. And as a reward, you put Harper Lee aside and check your email, only to find that your dissertation director has sent you an urgent message, asking you to meet him at a coffee shop in the union. He says something incoherent about a problem with the prospectus, so you put on your Goodwill coat and your Wal-Mart hat and start the mile-long walk back to campus.

Though it's a research one school, it's also a commuter school, and campus is as deserted as it was after the riots your first year in the program. You wonder for a moment if there is another living soul on campus, but eventually you find your dissertation director sitting at a table in an isolated corner of the union—far from the plate glass windows at the front and too far from the handful of other patrons for you to be comfortable, causing you to flash back to your second year in the program. The year you were his favorite, the year you went out for drinks after every class, the year he put his hand on your knee underneath a table littered with empty bottles and cigarettes, the year that hand stayed on your knee longer than it should have, the year you excused yourself and went to the bathroom in a pathetic but successful attempt to dodge his advances, the year the two of you stopped being friends.

But even though he's sitting in a cozy corner in the back of the coffee shop, even though no one else is around, you're not worried. He's long ago rejected you in favor of someone else, someone younger, someone prettier, something with bigger breasts. His new star. And you wonder if you were right to walk away, you wonder if it could have been *your* story in the *New England Review*. But no matter how intensely you long for that kind of success, no matter how many years—yes, years—it's been since you published your last story, you know that you'll always Leanne Womack it when it comes to selling out.

And your dissertation director knows that by now too. He knows you—your feminist leanings, your idealistic ideology, your old-fashioned desire for fidelity, your disgust with the old-boy network. Sure, he claims to be a feminist too, but that's all for show. Truth is, he'd rather see you barefoot and pregnant than standing in front of a classroom, and he will never take your stories about strong women seriously. Secretly he thinks they're funny. Even cute.

So you stride up to him with confidence, sure he can never break you. But then he does his best. He tells you that an April defense seems improbable, possibly even impossible, that your ninety-page novella has to be cut, that there's far too much work left on the other stories for you to graduate in the spring.

You remind him that these are the stories he "greatly admired" three years ago, the stories he said showed signs of real promise, even brilliance, but he balks. April is only six weeks away, he snorts. How can you possibly finish?

You want to smack him, to kick him, to slap him, but instead, you take in a long breath and consider your options. You know they are unlikely to give you another year of funding, and you know the interview well has dried up. You could cry harassment, but would anyone believe you? Would *you* believe you?

Still, you know he's not being fair, you know he's just trying to put the screws to you because you excused yourself and went to the bathroom that one night three years ago. So rather than lashing out, you decide to call his bluff. You remind him that the dissertation is supposed to be a *draft* of a publishable book, not the real deal, and that unlike some of your peers, you wrote something *entirely different* than the book that served as your Master's thesis, and then, just in case your words aren't all the convincing he needs, you add something else . . . a smile. Then you catch his eye and hold it. Come on, you say, you *know* I'm ready.

To your surprise, this works.

He smiles back at you, his eyes twinkle just a bit, and he says, Okay, but it better be air-fucking-tight. You assure him it will be and then head for the door before he takes your smile the wrong way.

Just to be sure he won't try to back out, you make a visit to your department chair the next day, the one who's married to a former grad student and sleeping with a current one. And you do something you almost never do . . .

You wear a skirt.

And knee-high boots.

With black stockings.

And you saunter into his office like the slut you used to be in college, all hip and ass because you don't really have the breasts. You tell him how excited you are about your defense, you tell him that your dissertation director has given you the go-ahead and how much you've appreciated his guidance over the past five years.

He is moved.

He blushes.

He looks at your knees.

When you get home, you confess everything to your husband. You've finally sold out, you tell him, and he says, it's about time. And then you get to work. You call MELUS and tell them you won't be able to deliver your paper in March, that you've got a deadline to meet. And you spend the next six weeks doing almost nothing but revising—you consider every word, every comma. You cut, you add, you paste. You re-write and re-think and re-vamp. You get so behind on your movie viewing that you haven't seen half of the films that win on Oscar night. You've cancelled classes so many times your students don't even remember your name. But you're not giving up. You're going to finish. No matter what anyone else does or says to try to stop you.

And somehow you do it.

You finish.

And except for the defense, you're done.

(And you don't know yet that those ninety minutes—when your dissertation director and his posse will come after you like Rummy on Hussein, like Smiley on Twain—will be their own private hell, so don't even worry about that. Keep telling yourself that the hard part is over, and by the time you realize— ten minutes in—that the defense isn't a gimme, you'll already be too close to the finish line to let anyone, especially a bunch of overeducated white boys, stop you.)

And so it happens. Even your dissertation director is satisfied with your revisions. Or maybe he just wants to get rid of you—it's hard to tell, but you don't even care anymore. Your principles are out the window. You just want the degree whether you've earned it or not.

To celebrate, you go to the graduate recruitment party at the department chair's house, where next year's class is being wooed with free beer and face time with the luminaries, most especially your dissertation director who gets so drunk he trips over a chair and does a face plant at the feet of a new admit, a faux pas that is easily overlooked because everyone is so busy talking about the two third-years doing it in the laundry room.

When you meet the new recruits, try not to notice that one of them (the bleached blonde one) dresses like a stripper, that another (the one with long brown hair that whips her ass like a pony) can't pronounce the word "rhetoric" without putting the accent on the second syllable, and that yet another (this one with flowing red locks) goes by the name of Cherry but spells it with a double E, not a Y—"Cherree." Consider them third-wavers who are broadening the definition of what it means to be an intellectual. Think of them as Charlie's Angels with books instead of guns. And *don't* think about whom they might have slept with to get in, and whatever you do, do *not* spend *one single second* worrying about the standards of the program or what your degree will be worth when you finally get it. And don't *even* consider thinking back to the people from Iowa who quit your program at the end of your first year in a cloud of elitism and Patchouli, saying that a degree from your school would embarrass them.

No, don't think about any of that.

Just have another beer and be happy. Because you're almost there. You're almost finished with all of it. With the quid pro quo and the nepotism and the scratching of backs and the backstabbing and the beast with two backs.

All of it.

And don't forget that when it's all finally over, they will have no choice but to call you "doctor."

Doctor!

And, no, that won't *really* matter to you. But it will mean something to your parents, your in-laws, your jealous brother, your peers, your BFF and her loser ex-boyfriend, even Charlie's Angels will be impressed, and knowing that it means something to them might mean a little bit to you.

Of course, when all is said and done, that piece of paper really will mean nothing—well, not nothing, but very little. And you will think far too often about the time you've lost—seven years of your life!—instead of what you've gained. Seven years wasted writing prospecti and grading papers and sucking up to old perverts when all you wanted to do was write, when you never loved language or metaphor the way they told you should, when all you cared about was telling stories.

But later—maybe months later or maybe years—it will hit you . . . *this* is a good story. *This* is a story I want to write.

And then, without really even knowing what you're doing, you will sit down at the computer your proud parents gave you for graduation, and you will—for maybe the first time in your life—finally start to write.

Look Away

My brother Andy ironed his collar with his shirt still on, leaving a scar on his neck that looks like a caterpillar. He'd landed a new job at the Big Lots uptown and wanted to look fancy. Andy is the oldest boy but only third in a line of six.

Jeannie was the first. She works for a dentist and believes in commercials: if she sees it on TV, then it must be true. Andy calls her a zombie, but he watches too.

Next is Rosie. She does three hundred sit-ups a night and circles her eyes with fat blue liner. Everyone says she'll be pregnant by the end of sophomore year.

Martin, the youngest, plays dress-up with our cousin Jessica: stained red lips and purple feather boas that used to belong to Rosie.

They all think Henry is weird. He likes to read and stay inside all summer.

My mother teaches special ed. She calls her students retards, but insists, "I'm the only one who can say that" when Martin protests and Henry gives her a dirty look. She settled for Dad when she was two months pregnant with someone else's kid. Jeannie doesn't know he isn't her real father.

Dad eats with his mouth open, and Mom has given up on telling him to shut his trap.

I just look away.

Me, I'm the only normal one. I figured out how to beat the system: how to get boys off without getting knocked up, how to earn good grades without cracking a book, how to convince Dad to give me his loose change.

I'll be gone by the time Martin comes out of the closet and Rosie's given birth, before Henry kills himself and Jeannie cries herself to sleep. Before Andy sets the house on fire. I'm saving up for a ticket to Los Angeles. I get the boys at school to pay me when I'm nice to them. The teachers give the most: one time, fifty bucks. By the end of the school year, I'll have enough to make it three months.

I don't want to be a superstar or a model or anything stupid like that. I just want to be different than my family. I want to leave them behind and never come back.

I want to be new.

The Lake in Winter

I had the feeling that the world was left behind,
that we had got over the edge of it,
and were outside man's jurisdiction...
Between that earth and that sky
I felt erased, blotted out.
I did not say my prayers that night:
here, I felt what would be would be.

—WILLA CATHER

Ty isn't Violet's boyfriend—just the boy she's sleeping with. He's the cutest one she's ever had, and Violet knows she's nothing special. For nearly a month, they've been parking in Ty's new sky-blue Chevy pickup on weeknights when there's nothing else to do. They drive out to the empty field behind the small airport on the north side—the nice side—of Coldwater, and Ty pulls her to him.

Before they start, Violet watches the barely visible outline of the small airstrip and hopes the runway lights will illuminate, the sign that a nearby plane is approaching. But most nights the tarmac stays dark.

After they are finished, Ty lets his head fall in her

direction, and they sit for a few minutes without speaking. In the dashboard's faint gold light, Violet is able to study Ty's face. Dark stubble grows against the green pallor of his winter skin. His profile reminds her of an old-time movie star: the silhouette of his strong jaw line pronounced in the near dark. She knows that if he were to turn and look at her, his thick eyebrows would stretch across his forehead in perfect arches and his dark eyes would take her into their depth, overwhelming her until she couldn't look away.

Sometimes she lets herself reach out and brush her hand against the small hairs along the back of his neck. She could look at him all night if he'd let her, but instead she takes what she gets without complaint: a sly smile when he picks her up, some friendly words on the drive out of town, the gentle caress of his hands on her body, and this—a few moments to enjoy his company.

Violet is just average, and for her, a special boy comes around only as often as the seasons. So she feels like Ty is a prize, something to be cherished. She's desperate to hold on to him. Even if she can't do it in public. Even if almost no one else knows what they do. This means she goes along with him no matter how far across the line he travels. In the few weeks that Ty has been taking her to the airport, he has taught her to go further than she's ever gone before, but the night in the ice-fishing shack is something entirely different.

Ty shows up at her bedroom window just after eleven on a Tuesday night in mid-January with Roger Sanderson by his side. January nights are uncomfortable in most of the places that Violet has been to, but in Coldwater, Indiana, the weather is scalding—the kind of cold that makes the ends of your toes freeze no matter how many pairs of wool socks you have on. The kind of cold you don't go out in unless there's something in it for you. The kind of cold that gives a town its name.

Violet can tell Ty has been drinking when she first sees his face through the glass. She can't smell the alcohol on his breath yet, but she knows from the way he stares—without looking away from her gaze and as if he's not ashamed of her—that as soon as she steps through the window and into the snow, leaning into his solid frame for support, the bitter smell of liquor will attach itself to her. Because of this, because it is late even for him, she wonders if he is looking for trouble. Or maybe he just wants to have a little fun. With Ty, she can never be sure.

Roger Sanderson stands next to Ty, looking utterly chilled and a bit nervous. His pale skin has evolved to an electric shade of pink, and he wears a taut grin. She wonders what Ty has told him, what she might be getting herself into. She hesitates as she considers Ty's tendency to exaggerate. But then she realizes who she's dealing with: Roger Sanderson was one of the most popular students at Coldwater High when he graduated the year before. He was on the basketball team and the homecoming court.

Lately she's heard rumors about Roger—how he comes home from school every weekend, how he'll never be as big in college as he was in high school. But Violet and her friends don't usually go out with boys like Roger even though they get invited to all the big parties. So when Ty and Roger knock on her window, Violet hesitates for only a moment. She thinks about the wind chill being five below, about what time she has to be up for school the next morning, about her fear that Ty may have promised Roger more than she can deliver.

But, ultimately, she decides she has no choice but to go with them.

The three of them line the front seat of Ty's pickup, Violet squeezed between them like a child. They drive away from her house and all the other houses that sit on the water. For a time, no one speaks, and Violet looks out the foggy windshield for a distraction.

The frozen lake draws out beside them, a vast and untouched desert of blue-white snow, its beauty enhanced in spite of the desolate nature of the season. The emptiness of the landscape appears to lead to nowhere, and Violet studies it—in awe of this, her world—as if she is seeing it in a picture or on television.

When they park and get out of the truck, the ice is flat and smooth underneath their feet—it's been eight inches thick since Christmas. Ty strides across the frozen lake as if he is on skates, eventually dropping to his knees so that he can slide the rest of the way to his dad's ice-fishing shack. Snow flies in a small wake around him. The effect is so graceful that it makes Violet long for sleep, a thought that lingers until Roger grabs her hand and leads her across the ice as if they are as comfortable with each other as old friends. They follow Ty, slipping and grabbing at each other to keep from falling.

Inside, Ty lights an oil lamp on the shelf next to the door, and Roger pulls out a leather flask. Even within the four paneled walls, the cold is biting, and they have to drink Southern Comfort to keep warm, laughing about how crazy it is to be out this time of year.

It surprises Violet that it takes Ty twenty minutes to work up the nerve to say something about what's going to happen next, and when he eventually does, he just blurts it out.

"Want to get naked, Violet?"

He passes the flask to her again, and she can feel his eyes searching her as she throws a drink back. She glances in his direction, and he grins at her. This grin is the reason why she's here, why she can never refuse him. She doesn't respond to the question. She wants to pretend to be shocked, even though she knows it's what they had in mind all along, why they came to *her* window.

She waits for Ty to flinch or take back what he has said. To chicken out. She doesn't know which part of the situation is harder to accept—that she and Ty are not alone or the fact that he has put words to his desire, to *their* desire. But Ty doesn't flinch. He continues to stare at her, to take her—*all* of her—in. She can tell he's trying to persuade her with his attention.

Without really understanding why, Violet starts taking off her clothes. First she unlaces her sneakers, kicking one and then the other off by pushing the opposite toe against each heel. With a shrug, she knocks off her oversized parka, letting it fall behind her on the bench she's sitting on. Then she stretches out of her red rag-wool sweater and plaid flannel shirt, leaving her white turtleneck in place.

After she has stood, quickly pushed her jeans down around

her ankles, and carefully stepped out of them, she sits on top of her parka and sets about the more self-conscious task of removing her undergarments. She does this part slowly, careful not to reveal too much too soon. She removes her bra without taking off her turtleneck like she's learned to do in gym class— pulling the straps out through the arms one at a time. Then she lifts her knees up to her face and wiggles methodically out of her underwear, letting the front of her turtleneck fall in front of her body like a curtain.

Except for her thick gray socks, Violet is naked. She can tell that Ty and Roger can't believe it any more than she can, but she isn't about to let them know she's afraid. And she isn't going to let an opportunity like this pass her by either. So they all sit there for a moment, avoiding each other's eyes, not sure what to do next.

Eventually Ty looks at Roger and takes charge of the situation. "What are you waiting for, Sanderson?" he says.

Roger stands up from his position on the floor of the opposite wall and approaches Violet. Carefully, he sits on the bench beside her, as if the plywood might give under his weight, and she moves over to make room for him. Violet senses that, like her, he is torn between not wanting to do anything and not wanting to look like a coward. Realizing this, she takes pity on him. She reaches over and unzips his fly, causing Roger's erection to grow and stretch against the white fabric of his long johns. He turns to touch her, but before he can do it, Ty begins to taunt him.

"I thought you wanted to get her from behind, Sanderson."

Roger sighs and shakes his head at the ground. Violet wonders what he's thinking and how much of what Ty says is the truth, how much they've planned things out beforehand. Roger lifts his head to look at Ty and laughs. It's not a normal laugh, not the kind that escapes you when you hear a joke, but the kind of short, unconvincing laugh you let out when you know you have no choice but to give in.

And then Roger pulls Violet in his direction so that she has to stand in front of him. He gently presses on her from behind until she realizes he wants her to get down on the floor. A braided oval rug lines the ice, and Violet can feel the dampness of its fibers against her bare legs as soon as she kneels.

Roger lifts his right leg over Violet and lowers himself onto the ground behind her. He puts his hands on either side of her waist and points her body in Ty's direction, positioning her between the two of them like a buffer. She leans forward, now on all fours, and lets her head drop, as if to inspect the navy-and-tan rug. The crooked weave tells her it was made by hand, probably a gift from a grandmother or an aunt.

All the while she is aware of Roger behind her, taking down his pants, rubbing his hand roughly against himself, and finally leaning into her. Violet feels the acid in her stomach rise up and mingle with the saliva at the back of her throat. She holds her breath and waits for the sensation to pass and for what she knows will follow, coaxing herself to accept it.

She closes her eyes and wills herself to think of something warm. Her mind cooperates: she imagines sinking into a tub full of steaming bath water, her body slowly immersing itself.

Without realizing it, Violet starts swaying back and forth against Roger's frame. She can feel that Roger is hard, and she prepares for what comes next, willing herself to relax. But Roger pushes himself inside too fast, rocking against her body rhythmically, as if he doesn't know anyone else is there. Violet opens her eyes and sees Ty watching, his hand on his jeans. She squeezes her eyes shut and tells herself it will be over soon, that she must be more than halfway there.

Even with her eyes closed, she can sense that Ty is becoming irritated, impatient. She can hear his breathing, hurried and loud, underneath Roger's grunting. She knows Ty well enough to know he doesn't like to wait, that he won't be able to stand it much longer.

"What is wrong with you?" he asks her, putting words to his frustration. Violet's eyes flash open at the sound of his voice. It's not a question she is expected to answer, and he yells at her instead of waiting for a response: "Hurry the fuck up!"

Why is he blaming her?

He continues to glare at them, and his body leans towards her aggressively as if he wants to fight, the skin on his face taking on the blotchy crimson of a fever. He is watching at such close range and with such intensity that she feels as if he is critically aware of every touch, every breath. She is worried he can tell she's not concentrating hard enough or doing it right. She wants to help Roger find a slower rhythm, so she drops her head and tries to resist his thrusts with her hips, but he doesn't respond.

She looks up at Ty to see if her efforts have eased his frustration, but before she can catch his eye, a glint of light flashes off of his class ring, and the back of Ty's hand connects with her unprotected face.

Through the skin of her jaw, she can feel the metal knock her teeth, and the strength of his blow whips her head back against Roger's shoulder. The sting reverberates through her body in a wave. It feels as if someone has wiped sandpaper across her skin. This awakens something in her. The heat, the pain. The unexpectedness of it. It causes her to let go, to give up.

Ty yells again, instructing her to roll over. Roger and Violet shift at the same time: he releases her, and she turns in a semicircle, as if they are used to repositioning themselves together, and the dampness of the grooved rug against her naked back causes the unpleasant sensation of moisture to pass through her.

She reaches up toward Roger, and this time she does not resist him as he slides inside her. They start moving back and forth together. She grips Roger's shoulders to draw him nearer. She feels suddenly as if she can't get him close enough, as if they can never be as tight as she desires. She is aware of pulling on his dense body, reveling in the feeling of his strength and exertion.

When he is finished, she leans her head back and rests, holding onto Roger's frame loosely and taking comfort in the now full weight of him on top of her.

But before she can catch her breath, Ty is there, yanking Roger off of her, forcing him to slide out of her with a wet pop. Even though she knew this was coming, that this was part of the plan, Violet winces when Ty unbuckles and drops his jeans to the floor.

With a quick pull on his shorts, Ty finishes undressing, and his penis makes its way out. He steps toward Violet. Her words—"No" and "Wait"—float past him and do nothing to slow his forward motion.

As Ty kneels and pushes on top of her, Violet becomes aware of how dry, how tender, she has become. When he forces himself in, it feels to her as if he has opened her up completely, as if he has taken over her being and is obliterating her insides piece by piece. Roughly and mechanically he repeats his movements. She has no choice but to lie there and yield to him, unable to pretend anymore that this is what she wanted.

When Ty is finally done, he is back on his feet in seconds, pulling up his pants and glowering down at Violet like he is disgusted with her. He glances to his right and sends the same expression in Roger's direction.

Violet follows the path of Ty's gaze and notices Roger sitting on the floor in the corner. He looks empty to her, as if he too has felt something inside of him give way. His pants are still down, his shriveled penis still visible.

Violet starts to tremble, and she is suddenly aware again of the frigid night air. She wants to get out of there—out of the shed, away from Ty and Roger—and home to the comfort of her soft pillow and the security of her own bed. And even though her limbs have begun to ache, she wills herself to get up and dress as quickly as she can. When she's put herself back together, she hurries out the flimsy wood door, letting it slam behind her and leaving any discussion inside with the two of them.

Outside, the night sky is as clear as it is cold, and the stars appear infinite—like thousands of eyes watching her from every direction. Tomorrow she will want the attention, she will even court it. But tonight, she turns away from it, focusing instead on her blue sneakers.

She imagines she is a child again—on the ice for the first time—and pretends she cannot catch her balance, that her feet are not steady. She gives in to this feeling of helplessness, allowing it to take her over. Her rubber soles slip and skate on the ice below her as she gets lost in the space of her mind and patiently waits for Ty to take her home.

Himmel und Erde

For Mike Silverman

S hrouded in yards of barbed wire and chain-link fencing
on both sides, the graffiti-covered wall was virtually
hidden. I caught only a glimpse of it when I crossed its
threshold, so afraid was I to glance above the heads of the
guards, and I was through the checkpoint before I realized I
had not made a clear imprint of it in my memory despite the
fact that I had studied its facade on the news many times
before. I was almost twenty-six and traveling with my friend
Sarah, visiting the place her family had come from. At the last
minute, Sarah had convinced me to spend the day in East
Berlin even though that part of the city had not been included
on our original itinerary.

Erik and Sheldon—two of Sarah's friends—met us outside
the secured area. Standing in a snow bank, their faces were
flushed to an unnatural shade of pink. It was December, the
cold and wind more bitter in that part of Europe than it was
even back in northern Indiana where I had grown up wearing
a hat and mittens well into April.

Erik hugged Sarah, playfully kissing her all over her face,

which caused her to giggle and blush, unusual behavior for a person usually defined by coolness and affectation. In contrast, Sheldon's embrace of Sarah was awkward, his kisses on either side of her face obligatory. Men didn't normally hold Sarah at such distance.

Even I had to admit she was striking. Not in the usual Jewish way, not because of skin so pale that it seemed to disappear under your gaze. Rather she was luminous, a negative version of the typical California girl but equally radiant. Her dark hair caught the light in an unusual way—reflecting rather than absorbing it—causing gold glints to sparkle off of her thick, black curls. It was this sense of radiance, along with the pale auburn freckles crawling across her nose like stars, that forced people to revel in her beauty.

I am not so lucky. For every part of Sarah that shines, I have a part that is equally dull. My flat, dirt-colored hair hangs around my shoulders in uneven, nearly transparent strands. My empty gray eyes look at me every morning in the mirror and beg for more.

More beauty, more vitality.

More.

Sarah took more in thick fistfuls—like the grass I used to tug out of the ground behind my parents' farmhouse—and I wanted to be able to do that, to take and to have, as well as Sarah did.

In the three years I had known her, Sarah had taken whatever she could get: she had hijacked opportunities that were not hers, appropriated relationships that even *she* couldn't argue she had a right to, and abducted people who belonged to others. I was no exception to this rule—she had stolen as much from me as she had from anyone.

But I wasn't angry.

No, I admired Sarah. I wanted to learn how to grab at life like it was a possession, something to be held, which I suppose was why we were friends and why I was there, following Sarah's lead and finding my way in her world. In the home of Sarah's history, it was my hope that I would be able to take a little bit back from her.

Sarah stepped away from Sheldon and held her arms out in my direction, presenting me like a Thanksgiving turkey and jarring me from my thoughts. "Erik, Sheldon," she announced, "this is Janie." Erik lunged forward and pulled me into an embrace, showering me with almost as much warmth as he had just shown Sarah. Sheldon was more reluctant, putting his hands cautiously on my elbows and holding me at arm's length as he kissed the air on either side of my face.

Immediately I knew the trip had been a mistake.

First of all, Sheldon was tall.

Back then I didn't go out with tall men—too intimidating, I suppose. He was also thin, though not weak. Even in his bulky gray parka, I could tell—by his firm grip and intense posture—that he was strong and fit. All of that I could have ignored, but it was his chestnut-colored hair, hanging down to the bottom of his prominent jaw line like a woman's, that made me hate him. Sheldon was good looking, probably too good-looking for me, and he had to have been as aware of that fact as I was.

Then there was Erik.

Much shorter than Sheldon, he wasn't significantly taller than Sarah or me, and when he flung his arm around her shoulder as we strolled toward the city, his curly hair mingled with hers, making them look like they belonged together. Sarah hadn't told me much about Erik. Just that he was absentminded: he never remembered to call or write after her visits. But that didn't stop her from seeing him every year. Still, he clearly wasn't the kind of guy she went out with back home. Sarah tended towards men who displayed their wealth like hood ornaments: showy and up front. Erik, a musician, wore his hair long and his jeans frayed, making me question who Sarah became there, on the other side of the world.

At the same time, I could sense from the way they touched each other—with warmth but without passion or possession—that Sarah and Erik's affection for each other was more familial than romantic.

Sarah had met Erik while visiting her aunt the summer after college, engaging in a brief fling with him before admitting that neither one of them was looking for a relationship and predictably swearing to remain friends for the rest of their lives. Unlike most people, they had managed to keep that pact. She had told me all about their history, but until we were getting ready that morning, she hadn't mentioned her plans for Sheldon and me.

"You should have told me," I said to her reflection in the mirror rather than looking directly at her face.

"I wanted it to be a surprise, and besides, I didn't know if it would work out."

I had learned from experience not to trust Sarah's surprises, but instead of calling her on past mistakes, I opted for something more vague: "I didn't come here to meet anyone," I said, finally turning in Sarah's direction.

"Janie, Shel will love you! Besides, it's the only way to really see things. You have to experience it through *their* eyes." Sarah's tone told me I shouldn't try to argue with her, that we were doing things her way no matter what. So I didn't put up a fight. Not yet anyway. Instead I looked back at the mirror and tried to imagine what two strangers would see when they looked at a face that seemed incredibly uninteresting, even to me.

We made our way through an abandoned park along the Spree, a ghost town of wet gravel and dead weeds, before the four of us settled on lunch. At a café near the river, I sat next to Sheldon and could feel his arm brush up against mine every time he lifted his drink. By then I was certain he was ignoring me, so consistent was he about not meeting my eye or glancing in my direction. Instead he talked to everyone at once, only making direct contact with Erik and, on occasion, Sarah. My anxiety increased, and to cope, I kept to myself. But it wasn't long before Erik put me in the middle of the conversation.

"Janie, you like this?" he began, waving his hand theatrically at the café. I had noticed Erik enunciated his words carefully, articulating each syllable and rephrasing certain words mid-sentence. He also replaced his J's with a Y, pronouncing my name Yanie instead of Janie. And, unlike other Berliners we'd met earlier in the week, he never let himself slip into German with Sheldon or Sarah. "You like the service?" Erik asked, and Sheldon lifted his head and grinned in a way that said, *I know where you're going with this.* "Shel and I like it here. We think, too, the best way to understand a girl is to watch how she treats the service." Erik paused, allowing me time to consider the idea, but I wasn't sure what he meant. "Does she look the girl in the eye? Does she use her name? Does she say 'please' or 'thank you'? What character is she?"

"You mean what kind of character does she have?" Sarah asked.

"*Ja.*"

"But what if the service is lousy?" I asked.

"That is the question. She should treat bad service like it is good."

I had stopped eating to give Erik my full attention. He seemed to be singling me out, and I wanted to appear interested. I knew I should reply with something equally thoughtful, but all I could think about was whether or not I had been nice to our waitress earlier in the meal. I couldn't remember my own behavior, but the memory of Sarah snapping at the woman for bringing her a dirty glass ran in my head on a loop. "How smart," I said. My words came out before I could think of something more engaging to say.

"*Schnauze,*" Sheldon said simply, again without looking at me. And then he went on: "Insurance. It is insurance against girls beneath us." Sheldon took a casual bite of his sauerbraten, as if he wasn't interested in how we might respond. I was taken aback by his arrogance, and I couldn't help but wonder what Sarah had been thinking when deciding to set us up.

Although Sheldon was oblivious, Erik registered my disgust. He said, "No, Janie"—my name again becoming Yanie in his mouth, a revision that thrilled me—"this is not bad, only protection. Insurance from getting hurt. Everyone must do it."

"Not me," Sarah said. "I have no idea how to protect myself. I always get the bad boys."

"But you like it that way," I said to Sarah suddenly.

"See how they treat the service," Sheldon said to Sarah. His words came out firmly, as if he were giving her instruction.

"Oh, I don't mind," Sarah said. "I never let them get away with it, do I, Janie?" Sarah looked at me, and I knew she was thinking of all the men she had held onto just long enough to enact her revenge.

"No, you never let anyone get away with anything," I said without thinking.

Sarah glared at me, letting me know that my voice had betrayed more disapproval than intended. Then, as if it were some kind of reproach, she asked, "So how did Janie do, Erik? Did she pass your test?" I was sure that Sarah's question was a punishment, so when Erik took a deep breath, as if working up the nerve to respond, I winced. But Sheldon spoke before anyone else could.

"She has passed," Sheldon said simply, and then he added: "Flying colors, ja?" He allowed himself a small grin, as if he was impressed with his use of the language. I was irritated by how much he seemed to like himself, but more importantly, I couldn't fathom that the same person who only moments before had seemed so disinterested had given me such an unadulterated compliment. His approval was something I could not have predicted.

E rik and Sheldon took us on a tour of Weißensee after lunch. The sky had changed from gray to muddy green, making the city appear jaundiced. Though the sun was not visible, a brilliant copper light outlined the dark clouds. All of my nervousness had been washed away by the words Sheldon had spoken back in the restaurant: *flying colors*. Perhaps his comment had been simple honesty or maybe he was picking up on the tension between Sarah and me and trying to exacerbate it. Or—and this was what I wanted to believe—he had seen something in me, something most people don't.

No matter the reason, I found myself momentarily freed from my insecurities. It wasn't that I thought Sheldon was interested in me. Unlike Sarah, I had no expectations for the trip. It was just that I could stop worrying about whether he was counting the minutes until he could get away from me.

"The weather is best now," Sheldon explained as we glided over the top of a small hill where four connected lakes lay before us like an expanse of spilled ink.

"During winter?"

"Before winter," he said. "Before the cold gets bad. Now, it is warm enough for the world to look like that." I laughed at the idea that Sheldon thought the weather was warm, but he didn't seem to notice, instead pointing his chin to the sky: "The warm and cold meet." Rather than follow his gaze, I studied his profile. In the queer brightness of the afternoon, his face was stunning, almost statuesque.

Sheldon turned to me and said, "You are staring."

"What?" I asked.

"You are staring!"

"I guess I was. It's something about this light."

Sheldon turned back to the burning clouds. I looked around for Sarah and Erik and saw that they had fallen a block behind. "What's it like here the rest of the year?"

"There is no joy." He glanced at me and then let out an uncomfortable laugh. "Maybe I live here too long. Some say summer is beautiful. It is not easy for me to call it 'beautiful.' But it is to some. I do not like it when people visit and say their home is not so beautiful. I do not like that they do not appreciate where they are from. But I do the same thing."

"At least you're aware of it."

"And you? Do you like your home?"

The movement of Sarah's hand caught my eye, and I watched her accept the first drops of rain into her open palm. Sarah and I had met in Washington, D.C. three years before, only a year after I had moved there. The District was one of the most awe-inspiring places I had ever been. Nothing I had seen up to that point was as dramatic as the drive along the Virginia side of the Potomac at night. From across the river, each of the spotlit monuments appeared along with its twin reflecting off the water's gentle waves. But the longer I lived there, the more I longed for a simpler kind of majesty—like the sun setting over endless fields of corn.

"I do," I said. "I never did before. When I was a kid, I hated the unrelenting monotony of the Midwestern landscape. I thought if I had to pass through one more cornfield, I would just die. But now . . . now I . . ."

"Hard to say?"

"Yes, hard to say."

Sheldon reached into the pocket of his coat and pulled out a pack of cigarettes. He lit one for me before taking one for himself. After taking a long inhale, he said, "Sarah never said you are smart."

"I'll have to remember to thank her." Apparently, Sarah had told Sheldon and Erik about me, but I had trouble imagining what words she would have chosen. "Unfortunately, she didn't tell me much about you—just how you met," I told Sheldon. "She didn't even mention we'd be seeing you."

"Sarah keeps secrets. We can too."

I laughed then, but I was happy that Sheldon understood Sarah's flaws as well as I did.

When the rain finally arrived, it didn't start slowly but rather came fully. We were still taking in the landscape the moment it hit, and even though we raced to the pub, our clothes were soaked through by the time we arrived.

Once we had shaken ourselves dry and were seated at a square table in the back of the bar, we drank our beers in silence, concentrating on getting warm rather than talking. But after the second round arrived, Sheldon spoke abruptly. "How did you become friends?" he asked us.

"Who? Me and Janie?" Sarah said but went on before he could answer. "Jane lives with my friend Karin. Erik, you've met Karin." Erik nodded at his beer. I knew Karin had traveled to Germany with Sarah before, but until that moment I hadn't known she had met Erik. Sarah continued: "Well, a few years ago, a bunch of us went skiing together—me, Karin, Jane, and some others. It was one of those perfect trips, wasn't it, Janie? The weather was amazing, and everything went right. Or at least *almost* everything." Sarah put her arm around my shoulder and leaned in close to me, as if she intended to tell me a secret. But instead, Sarah announced her crime to the whole table: "I stole Karin's date!" Sarah giggled shamefully, but I knew she didn't feel bad, that she never would, no matter how much she had hurt Karin. Sarah noticed my expression and added, "Oh, Janie, don't start." She shifted back to her own chair without removing her arm from my back. "He was all wrong for her."

"Only because you thought—for three whole nights—he was right for you."

"Sarah!" Erik exclaimed. "You *are* a bitch." But then he laughed, as if the way Sarah treated people were entertaining. Still, there was an edge in his voice, as if he too had been the recipient of Sarah's cruelty.

"You know you don't mean it," Sarah said to Erik playfully. In truth, she didn't mind people saying such things about her. She courted her bad reputation.

Rather than come to Sarah's defense, I went along with the joke. "That's what makes Sarah, Sarah," I said. "Anyway, she was right. Karin didn't need to worry about how he treated the help when he slept with one of her friends, did she?" Everyone laughed but me. I didn't bother to add that this was the same lesson I had learned from Sarah. It was six months after the ski trip when Sarah made her move on Clint, a lobbyist I had started to see a few weeks before. At first, I hated Sarah for what she'd done. I had decided to cut her out of my life, no matter how long she'd been friends with Karin. But when she treated me to an expensive dinner and proposed her theory—that she'd saved me from months of heartache—I reluctantly acquiesced, still eager to continue living in Sarah's light, to belong.

Erik raised his glass. "To sleeping with our friends' lovers," he said.

"I'll drink to that." Sarah raised her glass to the center of the table to meet Erik's. Sheldon shrugged and lifted his mug.

After I drank, I said, "I've got another." Sheldon looked up from his beer. I could see he was curious about what I would say. "To friends who set you up halfway around the world and don't even tell you about it." I knew I was being more bold than usual, but I felt liberated, and the beer only compounded that feeling.

"*Ja*, good, good," Sheldon said, and he commanded us to drink, again picking up his mug, but this time shoving it directly into Sarah's, causing the beer to spill over the side of her glass and onto the table. Rather than be offended, Sarah laughed and followed his orders.

Erik wiped his hand across his mouth and began to speak. "*Ja, ja,*" he said before pausing, as if practicing words in his head. "To friends . . . to friends who come around the world to fuck."

Erik's bluntness surprised me, but as we clinked our glasses, I looked at Sarah and noticed it didn't seem to faze her. "At least you're honest," I said, and Sarah giggled.

For a moment the revelry stopped, so we could catch our breath. Then Sarah pushed her chair back and stood up. She cleared her throat and said, "AND . . . to those who long for such friends to arrive but never remember to write after they're gone." We toasted again, and then Sarah leaned across the table, pulled on Erik's shirt with her free hand until he got up, and kissed him.

Sheldon and I watched until their lips parted. After Erik fell back in his seat, he turned to me and said, "I love Sarah."

"Who doesn't?" I asked.

"That is true!" Sheldon added with enthusiasm. "To all who have loved Sarah. And to those who will. Good luck to them."

"How appropriate," I said. I tipped my glass back and let the beer run down my throat until it was finished.

"Another?" Sheldon asked.

"Sure," I said.

While Erik and Sheldon went to the bar, I looked for a bathroom in order to avoid being alone with Sarah. Unlike American bars, the pub was brightly lit, making the customers look ashen and pale when I passed them on my way back. I wasn't used to seeing people's faces so clearly while I drank, and the effect was a bit sobering.

Back at the table, Sheldon pushed a shot glass in my direction.

"*Molle mit Korn*," he offered. "Beer and spirits, a tradition."

I obliged Sheldon's request. As I drank, I noticed that our group seemed more subdued than when we had split up a few minutes before. No one was talking, and I wasn't sure if I was expected to keep the silence intact. Finally, I managed to say, "So now that you know about us, what about the two of you? How did you meet?"

Erik grunted but didn't look up from his beer. Sheldon glanced at him, and when it was clear Erik wasn't going to respond, Sheldon said, "We live in the same building. In the Alexanderplatz."

"For how long?" I asked.

"For how long?" Erik said with a laugh, finally looking up from his glass. "Forever." His eye caught mine for just a second, and his face was so full of longing that it sent a flutter of emotion down my spine.

"It is where we were born," Sheldon explained. Erik dropped his gaze to his glass again, chuckled to himself. Sheldon leaned forward and put one elbow on the table, as if he were about to tell me something important. "We play together when we were little. We go to school together. Seems we spend all of our lives together."

"We do *not* work together." Erik raised his eyes once more. "Sheldon," he said, "is with the GDR." He hesitated. Then, before taking another sip of his drink, he added, "Shel is a traitor." Even though his words were harsh, Erik's tone didn't seem combative, as if he weren't insulting Sheldon as much as stating a fact.

"And so?" Sheldon asked. "I still live in the same building as you." Erik didn't respond, and Sheldon looked at me before he continued. "My parents . . ." he said, "they are deaf," pointing to his ear like it was an explanation though I didn't really understand what he was trying to say. I wondered what his parents' condition could have to do with his job, but my courage had dried up the last time I spoke, and I kept my question to myself.

"It is time to go." Erik stood up abruptly and reached over to help me out of my chair. I didn't hesitate to get to my feet.

Erik muttered something about going closer to home, and before I knew what was happening, we were boarding a bus marked "Greifswalder Straße."

Sarah took an empty seat, and I sat next to her. After we were settled, I looked directly at her for the first time since Karin's name had come up in the bar. "Where did your parents live?" I said, afraid to ask the question that was really on my mind. I knew Sarah's parents had fled to the United States just after she was born, but other than that, I knew nothing of their history.

"I don't know," Sarah replied without hesitation.

"You don't know?" I asked, skeptical.

Sarah looked out the window before she said, "They don't talk about it." Her voice was casual, nonchalant.

"And you don't ask?"

Rather than answer, Sarah shot me an annoyed look. I was well aware she had no desire to be interrogated. Every once in a while Sarah grew quiet, rare moments when she appeared almost disgusted—with herself or with someone else I could never be sure—and when she finally came out of her head, it was usually with more reticence and humility.

So rather than continue my line of questioning, I let Sarah slip off into her own world. And when I turned to check with Sheldon and Erik, they were slumped down in their seats, their eyes closed, two schoolboys on their way home from a long day of classes. I gazed out the window, enjoying the rhythmic hum of the engine and the scenery of a place that had previously been unknown to me.

After we got off the bus, the four of us walked through Volkspark Friedrichshain without discussing what was next. I knew from my travel books that it was Berlin's oldest park, but no one offered any commentary, and it didn't seem like the time to act like a tourist. Instead, I studied the monuments and the elaborate fountain we came across so I would not forget them as quickly as I had the wall that morning. And when we passed a small graveyard, I was surprised to see that it looked almost identical to one near my grandparents' farm: dingy gray headstones sprouted abruptly from the dying grass and scattered leaves.

We must have walked twenty minutes before Sheldon broke the silence. "Something to eat?" he asked.

Even though it still felt early, the sun was starting to set. I wasn't hungry and waited to see what Sarah would say, but she didn't speak or stop moving, as if focused on some unspoken destination.

"Sarah?" I said. She came to an abrupt stop then and turned to look at me. "Sarah, did you hear him?"

Sarah looked confused, but then she answered the question. "Yeah, sure, let's eat."

"We will find a café," Sheldon said and turned away from Erik, taking Sarah by the arm and leading her in another direction. As I followed them, a familiar feeling was building inside of me. Not hate exactly. Envy is what I suppose you would call it. But envy seemed like too benevolent a word. What I felt for Sarah was much stronger than envy. I thought of Karin, back in D.C. for the holidays, and wondered if she ever dreamed of getting back at Sarah. But Karin and I weren't really the types to avenge ourselves. We would bitch for hours about Sarah, but never once did we tell her how angry we were or do anything about it.

Following Sarah and Sheldon down the deserted path made me think the same thing all over again: *Sarah will never get it.* As long as I had known this—it had been over a year since the incident with Clint and maybe even longer since I had really understood this about her—I had never considered not being friends with Sarah, or saying, *Enough is enough, I'm done with you.* I knew this had something to do with why I had come to Germany, and I had some vague sense that I had made the trip out of spite. Might as well get something out of her, I figured.

Just then Sarah let go of Sheldon's arm and reached up to tousle his hair. He stopped walking and turned to face her. His smile seemed to convey appreciation, as if she had blessed him. It was a look of contentment, a look that said, *I know I'm loved.*

I was suddenly aware of Erik's presence next to me, and I wondered if he too was watching them, watching Sarah do her thing with Sheldon. But when I glanced at him, his face betrayed nothing.

Sheldon looked back at us and yelled: "Come along!" he said, waving his arm for us to follow, and we hurried towards them, obedient as pets.

W e ate dinner near the high-rise where Sheldon and Erik lived. The tiny tavern was named after a sausage dish called *Himmel und Erde* or, as Erik explained, "Heaven and Earth." Sheldon warned us away from ordering the sausage because it was served on a bland bed of pureed apples and potatoes. I ordered the Westphalia ham because it was the only thing on the menu I recognized. Sarah and Sheldon had currywurst, and Erik chose the Hassenpfeffer. Sarah and I cringed when Erik bit into a big hunk of rabbit meat, and he teased us by pushing his fork in our faces.

"The poor rabbit," Sarah said.

"Poor rabbit?" Sheldon balked. "The rabbit had a good life. He knows nothing of the world."

"He's blissfully ignorant?" I asked.

"*Ja*," Sheldon said.

Erik pointed his fork at Sarah. "Sarah, *mein Liebling*," he said, "why do you not eat?"

Sarah had been pushing meat around on her plate, but she had eaten very little. "I'm really not hungry."

"*Warum das?*" Sheldon asked, and I involuntarily flinched at the intimate sound of him talking to Sarah in German.

"Is it the Hassenpfeffer?" Erik asked her.

"It's not that."

I felt one of Sarah's moods coming on. Erik put his arm around her and pulled her close to him, kissing the top of her head.

"Then what?" Sheldon asked.

"It's silly," Sarah said, and Erik brushed his hand over her hair.

"*Bitte*," Sheldon insisted. The shortness of his delivery told me he was growing impatient.

Sarah lifted her face, and I couldn't tell if she was angry with Sheldon for pushing or glad that he wanted to know. "It's just hard to be here," she finally admitted. "Hard to leave. I wish we were staying longer."

"You have always known that," Sheldon said. "Why have regret now?"

"I just do."

Sheldon wiped his mouth with his napkin and then said, "I saw a film about a person like you, a doctor. All the time, the doctor acts without shame, but when others become hurt, he feels guilty."

I thought Sarah would be offended, but instead her eyes lit up. "*The Unbearable Lightness of Being*?" she asked.

"You know it?" Sheldon asked.

"Janie and I saw it last week," Sarah said. "I can't believe how right he got it."

"Who?" Sheldon asked.

"The director, whoever made that movie."

"How is that?"

"The sex," Sarah said. "The way a woman feels during sex. He got it exactly right." She stopped, and no one else spoke. "And that one scene—the one where she sleeps with the guy at the bar, you know, to get back at her husband? That was awful." Sarah ran her finger around the rim of her wine glass and went on. "That's exactly what it's like too. When a woman is with someone she doesn't want to be with. That's how it feels."

"It was her choice," Sheldon said.

"But she didn't really have a choice," Sarah asked, "Did she?"

No one responded, and I thought about what Sarah's motivations might be. She seemed genuinely upset, but I had seen that side of her before. The part of Sarah that made people feel like they had to reach out to her, to help her pick up the pieces. And I wanted no part of it anymore.

"But it is not real," Sheldon said. "They are just people Kundera made in his head."

"Shel, you are cold," Erik said, scolding his friend.

"And that woman, her suffering was not greater than others, was it?" Sheldon asked, ignoring Erik. He seemed to be turning away from Sarah and her charms somehow, as if he wasn't the same person who had only moments before been under her spell. Sarah had a way of wooing people with her attention and then driving them away with her self-centeredness.

"Maybe not," I said, curious about what Sheldon was trying to say. "But that doesn't make it any easier to watch."

"No?" Sheldon asked. "But evil, over and over, becomes easier to endure, no?"

"You mean you become desensitized?"

"That is what I am saying."

"Sure, but that's the point," I said. "You've got to force yourself to care. Every time you see a plane crash or an ambulance come down the street, you've got to remember that there are people inside. It could be *your* aunt being rushed to the hospital or *your* friend flying overseas." I stopped and looked at Sarah, pretending to be sympathetic before I went on. "And that could've been Sarah in that movie sleeping with the guy at the bar. I mean, how many times have you been to a bar with Sarah when she *didn't* go home with someone?"

"Jesus, Janie!" Sarah said.

"What's wrong, Sarah?"

"I was talking about something that mattered. Something important. I was affected by that movie."

"But, Sarah," I said, "when other people feel things, you don't care. Why should it be any different for you?"

"You're being so insensitive, Janie. Think about what I've been through." I knew Sarah wanted to make it seem like she'd been through something traumatic, but in truth, she hadn't experienced anything unusual. Like everyone else, she had, at times, put herself in a position she later regretted. Her suffering was not unique.

"What *you* have been through?" Sheldon asked in an accusatory tone. He leaned back in his chair before he continued. "Do you not understand, Sarah? You cannot sit here and cry to *us*." Sheldon motioned to Erik and to himself.

Sarah stared at Sheldon, clearly shocked by his attack, and I wondered if she thought he might apologize. When that didn't happen, she got up and started for the door. Before she got there, she turned to face the table and said, "Janie?" without looking up, as if commanding me to her side. I knew I was supposed to go with her, but I wasn't sure I could will myself to get up and leave. I told myself to act, but nothing came.

Erik pushed his chair back from the table. "I will go," he

said, saving me from having to chase Sarah. But before he left, he leaned over and whispered in my ear, "I will take care of her, and you will meet me later. At the news shop on the street—one o'clock."

Sheldon didn't ask what Erik had said. But after they were out the door, he added, "It is just as well. I have no ability to take her bullshit, you know?"

Outside of the restaurant, Sheldon grabbed my hand and pulled me into an empty alley. The touch of his skin, still warm from the restaurant, surprised me.

"You should have gloves," he said, but he didn't let go of my hand so that I could fish them out of my pocket. "I want to show you a place. But you must promise not to tell."

"Not even Erik?" I asked.

"No, not even Erik," he said. "It is a secret place." He winked, but then he explained himself: "Maybe I do not want Erik to know everything about me. I want to keep some things for just me, for us."

"I understand," I said, even though I was wondering exactly what he meant when he said, *for us.*

"This way," he said and pulled me down the alley toward a busy street. Sheldon held his hand up in the air, and eventually, an old, beat-up Mercedes pulled over. He leaned into the driver's window and spoke in a low voice. It was only the second time I had heard him use German, and I found myself taken in by the unique sound of his voice. Then he held the back door open, and I climbed in. The car was a diesel: it sounded like it needed a good throat clearing, and the engine shook so much that the seat vibrated underneath us.

"Where are we going?" I asked.

"To see the best Germany. To see the world."

When we got out of the car about twenty minutes later, I began to feel frightened for the first time that day. We were in a completely isolated part of the city, and after the car drove away, I couldn't imagine how we'd ever get back to Sarah and Erik.

Sheldon lifted his head toward the hill in front of us. I hadn't noticed it until then. "It is a good walk, okay?" he asked as he started towards an embankment with a steep groove. At the top of the slope, I could sense a stark light, but I couldn't make out where it was coming from.

"Come along," Sheldon yelled back at me. "You are here only a short time."

I caught up to Sheldon, and we walked in silence for the time it took us to climb the height of the small hill. At the top there were three wooden crosses planted in the middle of a grass circle, which sat on a cluster of concrete steps. The glow I had seen from the base below was a spotlight pointed toward the center cross. I walked around the circle and examined the crosses, careful not to get too close. It reminded me of the image I had created in my head of Mount Calvary.

"Calvary?" Sheldon asked. "Is that what you are thinking?"

"How did you know?"

"The Christians always frighten here—like they are seeing a ghost. It is certainly familiar."

"So what is it?"

"I cannot tell you." I turned away from the crosses and looked back to Sheldon, waiting for an explanation. He was standing at the edge of the precipice, smoking a cigarette and looking down the hill. "No one knows."

"What?"

"No one knows what this place is. Some say it is for the first three Jews lost in the war." I inspected Sheldon's face, looking for some sign of emotion, but I didn't know him well enough to read him. Then he shook his head. "But people would remember." Sheldon held his cigarette out over the cliff, let go of it, and watched it drop. He walked towards me as he went on. "Others think it is from the Crusades."

"Would it still be here?" I asked.

"It is doubtful. There are others—the most studied—who say they are the religions of Germany: the Christians, the Jews, the Muslims."

I looked back at the crosses and considered this idea.

"And you have not yet seen the best part. Come along." Sheldon walked up the steps to the base of the middle cross.

"Are you crazy?"

"No, I am not. This is the part that is best. Come." He held his hand out to me as if we were a couple, as if he reached for my hand all the time. I looked over my shoulder and cautiously walked up the white steps to the place where he stood. "Now, turn," he said, putting his hands on my shoulders and leading my body in the rotation.

When I spun around, I saw that—just twelve steps up from where I had stood before—the whole city of Berlin, East and

West, was before me, the houses and buildings washing into each other like a river, wave after wave of neighborhoods and parks spread out into a massive sea of gray concrete and dwindling lights.

"Look," Sheldon said, pointing. "There is the Nikolai-Kirche, the oldest church in Berlin. And there," he said, pointing in a different direction to a spot much father away, "the Kaiser-Wilhelm-Gedächtniskirche has been built again." He paused while I followed his finger. "What they say is that you can see all of the churches. That here we come together."

"It's perfect," I said.

"*Ja*," Sheldon said, "*himmel und erde*."

I turned to look at him as I translated the words in my head.

"A joke," he said before I could decipher his intent. "But it is like two worlds together, endless, though impossible."

Sheldon stared in the distance, not explaining himself further. Then suddenly he moved down the steps in the direction of the path, as if he didn't want to see what lay before us anymore. But just as suddenly he turned back and walked towards me, not stopping until he was within arm's length. Glancing at the ground, he began to kick the toe of his boot against the concrete steps.

I was wondering if I had lost him when he lifted his head and looked at me directly. "My hands," he said. "They are very cold." He moved closer to me and slid his bare hands into the pockets of my coat. I could no longer see the cloud of his breath as he exhaled.

I hadn't expected anything so intimate, but when it

happened, I wasn't surprised either. "This morning I didn't think you liked me," I said.

"This morning you were only the friend of Sarah. Now I understand: you see Sarah as I see Sarah."

"So you like me because I dislike Sarah?"

"I like you because you think your own way."

I knew he was wrong—I had been Sarah's shadow for so long it was hard to be sure who I was or what I did think. But at the same time, I understood that he saw something in me I had only recently come to recognize: I didn't want to do what other people expected of me any longer.

Sheldon went on. "What I do not like about Sarah is that she wants only the American thing." Sheldon looked over his shoulder. "Sarah is so American she probably has a Christmas tree." He laughed and turned his face back to mine. His hands were still in my pockets. "I am right?" he asked.

"As a matter of fact, yes."

"So you understand?"

"Christmas isn't all bad."

"Hanukkah is not bad either, but you do not celebrate, do you?"

I thought of the menorah I had made Karin the first year we lived together, the one I knew was, at that moment, sitting on our dining room table back in D.C. "No, not officially."

"So you see," Sheldon said with a shrug. "But what do you think of this?" He tilted his head towards the world behind him. "Are you pleased to see this?"

"Yes, I am very pleased," I said.

"And I am pleased," he said, looking directly into my eyes,

his attention almost too heavy for me to hold. I considered glancing away, but before I could, he leaned in to kiss me, and I let him do it. And even though I knew the light made us easy to see, it didn't feel like anyone was looking.

At the door to Sheldon's apartment, he looked back at me and said, "My parents are deaf. And they sleep early."

"I wanted to ask," I began, hesitating for a moment before finally being forthright, "what does your job have to do with them?"

Sheldon stopped in the middle of the hallway and turned to face me. "It is simple," he said. "Better doctors, better medicine, better—" Sheldon tapped his ear rather than finish his sentence.

"Hearing aids?"

"*Ja.*"

Sheldon's room was, strangely, very American. It reminded me of a college dorm. There was a sofa next to the bed and music posters on the walls. I sat on the sofa wondering what I was doing there.

When Sheldon walked across the room and sat next to me, I felt my body stiffen. "You are uncomfortable?" he asked.

"No, it's just . . ." I didn't know how to explain.

"Do not feel guilty. You are not the woman in the movie."

"I'm not sure I have a choice. It's just part of who I am."

"Why feel bad? You are smart. You know there is not a right time and a wrong time to have sex."

It was jarring to hear Sheldon be so frank about what was going to happen. There was no subtlety in his approach, none of the artificiality I had come to associate with such moments. "I bet you say that to all the girls," I said.

He laughed and said, "It would be clever." He stood up and walked over to the other side of the bed. A green plastic record player, the kind children usually have, sat on the bedside table, and he kneeled down to flip through some records on the floor. "The Jews think sex before marriage is good," he said a moment later.

"Are you being serious?"

"*Ja.*" Sheldon stopped talking and put an album on top of the turntable. After gently lowering the needle, the sound of David Bowie filled the room. It was the first non-German voice I had heard all day besides Sarah's. Once the music started, Sheldon walked back around the bed and stood in front of me. "Rabbis marry. Sex as bad is a Christian idea."

"Maybe you're just telling me this, so I'll sleep with you."

"But you have already decided to do so?"

I laughed and looked at the ceiling. He was right.

"I want you to have no guilt," he said as he sat down next to me on the sofa again, and for the first time that day, I was able to look directly in his eyes without looking away or getting nervous. "You want it. Why feel bad?"

"I'll see what I can do about it," I said as I reached up to touch his face.

Next to Sheldon's bed was an old alarm clock with the numbers that go around on a dial like an odometer. I was supposed to meet Erik in fifteen minutes.

"Sheldon, I've got to go," I said even though I knew he was

falling asleep.

"*Was?*"

"I've got to go." I got up from the bed and started looking for my clothes on the floor.

"But where?"

"To meet Erik. He said to meet him at one."

"Bullshit," he said, "you are not serious."

"Why not?"

"No, you cannot." I looked at him and tried to understand why he thought he could tell me what to do. "*Bitte—*" he began, as if rethinking his approach. "*Bitte,*" he pleaded. "Do not go to Erik."

"Why not?"

"Erik only wants to sleep with you." By this point, I had put my jeans and sweater on and was trying to find my boots.

"What are you talking about?"

"He wants you because I have you. He cannot let me have anything just for me."

"Well, why should you?" I asked. "Besides, you're the one who said sex was healthy." After I was finished getting ready, I went to the side of the bed and sat next to Sheldon. "I'm not going to sleep with him."

"Stay." Sheldon played with my hair as he spoke. "*Bitte,*" he said, and then, "Please. Please, do not go."

"I'm worried about Sarah," I said, even though I knew that wasn't the only reason I was going.

"*Ja,* go. Sleep with him. But tell him you were with me."

Though Sheldon's words were childish, even shocking, I understood them. "I have to go," I said.

"I will not see you again."

I looked at him, waiting for an explanation.

"You leave in the morning, and I must work."

"Why don't you visit us? We'll be here all week."

"Not possible, Janie." My name—Yanie—sounded so lovely in his mouth I did wish I had the courage to stay. As he gently stroked the side of my face, I was about to ask why he could not visit, to argue that I didn't know if I'd ever come back to Germany again and that whatever he had to do, he should get out of it. But then I remembered: it wasn't that he didn't want to visit, it was that he wasn't allowed to leave.

"Oh, God, Shel," I said. "I'm sorry. I forgot."

"You can do that—forget," he said, letting his hand drop to the bed and making me feel as if I had already left.

Erik was waiting at the door of the apartment building for me. He embraced me when I walked out, as if he hadn't just seen me a few hours before.

"Where's Sarah?" I asked as soon as he let go of me.

"She is asleep in the apartment. She is fine."

"Oh."

"I am hungry," he said. "Do you want to eat breakfast?"

"It's one in the morning."

"I feel as if I have not eaten all day. Come along."

"I don't know."

"What else can you do?" Erik asked.

I tried to picture myself going back to Sheldon's apartment, but I knew it was too late. I had already left him behind.

"We will eat and then you can wake Sarah. There is

no reason to sleep. You will only be here one day in your whole life."

"You never know," I said.

"I do know. You will not come back. Why would you?" He put his arm around my shoulder and led me away, and for some reason, I didn't resist.

E rik ordered an omelet with toast, and I just asked for coffee. I noticed that he cut his eggs with a knife and fork, even though he could have gotten by with only the one utensil. He ate for a while before he said anything. He seemed to be considering his words. It was a noticeable change from his gregarious demeanor earlier in the day.

"I love Sarah," Erik said finally. "She is beautiful, and she never forgets me. You know she always writes, she always visits?"

"I know," I said as I played with the ceramic salt and pepper shakers.

"Short visits," Erik said, "but I enjoy it every year. I do. Because we do what we like. No rules, no . . . what is it called? Expectations?"

"None?"

"Well, it is not possible to have none, but is not the same as with girls here. If I date a girl here, I am always thinking, is this good? Do I like her? Does she like me?"

"How does she treat the help?"

"Ja! And Sarah, I do not have to worry about it because there is no tomorrow. We are only happy together. That is all."

"So this year was a failure?"

"Sarah is not happy. Things did not go as we planned. I wanted Shel to have you like I have Sarah—one day every year, one day to forget."

It hadn't occurred to me that our setup had been as much for Sheldon as it had been for me.

Erik continued. "But I did not plan it right. You will not come back. You and Sarah might not even be friends. And Shel. He could never enjoy just one day. He is different than us. He is rigid."

"He seems pretty free to me," I said.

"*Ja*, well, it is an act." Suddenly Erik set down his knife and his fork. He looked at me and said, "You did not sleep with him?" And then: "I hope you did not sleep with him."

"Why not?"

"Because you are good. You are alive, you are free and open. Shel thinks there must be an answer to all questions. He thinks too hard." Erik paused for a moment and seemed to be waiting for my response. "He is my friend, but you do not want that."

"I don't have to want it if, as you say, I am never coming back."

"Maybe, but still." Erik flipped his fork over in has hand. "I am jealous you slept with him."

I was shocked to hear Erik admit this. "What about Sarah?" I asked.

"Sarah is my friend. She is my family." Erik hesitated. He leaned across the table and added softly, "She is asleep." He laughed at this, and I couldn't help but laugh too. The situation was completely absurd and yet exactly as Sheldon had predicted. I had just slept with Erik's best friend, and yet he was coming on to me. So why was I intrigued?

"So that makes it okay?" I asked.

"Do you care? Is this not what you want?"

"I'm not sure." I was just as surprised to hear Erik articulate some understanding of my situation with Sarah as I had been to hear him say he was jealous of Sheldon.

"You should have seen your face this morning!" he said.

"What did I look like?"

"You looked frightened. Amazed. You had never seen anything like that *verdammt* wall."

When I thought about that morning, my memory of the wall was eclipsed by the image of Erik and Sheldon standing on the other side, waiting for us to cross over. Everything was a blur of barbed wire and graffiti. "I don't even remember it," I said. "Isn't that awful?"

"I am not surprised. You have changed."

I thought of the events of the past day, Sheldon back in his room—the posters on the wall, the children's record player, a life he was not meant to live.

"Do you think it will ever come down?" I asked, hoping Erik would know what I meant.

"Does it matter, Janie? We can never go back."

Though I knew Erik was right, I couldn't help but wonder if I'd someday want to go back to the way things had once been, the way I had once been. Before I could answer that question, Erik took my hand and tugged gently.

"Let's go," he said. "We'll make certain."

"Of what?" I asked even though I already knew.

"Sarah," he said without explaining further.

And when he stood up from the table, I stood too, following him willingly out the door.

Sliders

It was Memorial Day, and I was pregnant.

My grandmother and I had just returned from Hickle's Hamburgers where we got carryout for lunch. We were sitting on her porch out back, eating greasy burgers Hickie called sliders. I'd taken to them as a kid, but now I only tolerated them because they were Grandma's favorite. I'd often suggested trying something else, but she always resisted.

We ate quietly, my grandmother poking questions at me now and then, about baby names and the like. I asked some questions too, easy ones to loosen her up. I was trying to find out what she thought about my "situation." She responded in her usual manner: abrupt, ending each sentence with a kind of half-nod and "The Look," her special form of punctuation.

The nod was an old habit, born of years gazing down her nose at her children and their children too, but The Look was more intentional. It was her way of making sure you were paying attention, and God help you if you weren't. After a few nods and several Looks, I let some time pass without words so I could work up the courage to ask her something I'd been wondering about lately: why she had waited thirteen years to have her second child, my Aunt Collette.

"Well, you know, I had three miscarriages between your mother and Collette," she said.

I hadn't known this, but I didn't think she was expecting an answer, so I just nodded back at her.

"Well, yeah, Henry and I had seven children, but only four of them lived. It was common. It *is* God's natural way of selecting, you know? There's no reason for us to start deciding now what God's been doing for us all along."

I stopped chewing. My slider didn't taste right anymore. I looked at the pile of ketchup on my plate and wondered if there was any way to spit it out without my grandmother noticing. I put the napkin up to my face, pretending to wipe it off and let the meat fall into my hand.

"That's awful," I said.

"No," she said firmly and gave me The Look, as if to say, *Didn't you hear what I just said?* I put my napkin down on my paper plate and turned the awkward bulk of my body to face her, so she would know I was listening.

Finally, she went on.

"We knew it was what God wanted and that was just the way things were," she said, her eyes staring into mine. Unwilling to be shaken off, I held her glare until she looked away to light up a cigarette. "The first two after your mother were miscarriages," she said. "The third was almost a stillborn." She stopped for a moment, as if to remember. "I didn't know what was happening. I thought I just had to go to the toilet." She laughed. "But when I got there, blood and fluids came out all over the place. Then I knew something else was coming, so I reached my hand down and wouldn't you know, there it was . . . so small, it fit right into my hand." She held her palm out in front of her and curved it carefully like she was holding something precious. "With its tiny feet dropping off at my wrist."

She put her other hand inside the open palm and made a fist. Then she unrolled the fist and let her fingers hang off the edge of her palm imitating little feet. I could see the fetus, small and wet, in her hand.

"So, I pulled my pants up, and carried it into the bedroom. Henry took a look and said, 'Why, Nellie, what have you got there?'"

She looked up at the sky, her eyes shining in the sun.

I was surprised she appeared so content. "So what happened?" I asked, reaching over to touch her arm.

She turned quickly, looking at me like I was a stranger.

"What happened with the baby?" I asked again.

"Oh," she said, coming back to the present. "It was too late. Like I told you, that kind of thing didn't matter. It was God's will."

I picked our paper plates up off the table and walked to the kitchen. My plate was destroyed—the ketchup had eaten a hole through it—while my grandmother's plate looked untouched, as if it hadn't even been used.

"Aren't you going to finish your slider?" she asked me.

"No," I said as I lifted the lid of the trash can and dumped the used plates inside. "I don't want it anymore."

Missionary Work

Dear Abby,

I'm writing because something has happened to me, something surprising and enormous, and I'm not sure what to think about it, much less do.

They always say it's best to start at the beginning, so that's what I'll do . . .

Last weekend my husband and I took our two perfect children to my parents' summer house on Chesapeake Bay, just over an hour from our home in Georgetown. We have an adorable six-year-old daughter—whose saucer-like blue eyes and shiny blonde ringlets capture the heart of every little boy she meets—and a sweet-as-sugar two-year-old boy who is becoming more and more like his big, strong daddy every day. Abby, I have to tell you that just writing about my babies here makes me feel so completely fulfilled and content that I can't even imagine why I'm telling you all of this.

But I believe that secrets are as close to sins as one can come, so I feel I must unburden myself.

It was a gorgeous Saturday morning when we left town—the heat that had all but ruined the rest of August had just broken, and we were able to roll down the windows of the minivan and let in some of God's glorious air. My husband—I'll call him Taylor—had to come back early on Sunday for a meeting at work. I don't know anyone else who works on the Lord's day, Abby, but Taylor has a weekly strategy meeting every Sunday afternoon. It's not what I would call the Christian way of doing things, but Taylor is the one who supports this family so I go along.

The point of all this is to say that we had to take two cars. Me: I rode in the minivan with the children. Taylor was alone in his Beamer—technically that's my car because Daddy gave it to me when I graduated from college seven years ago, but I let Taylor drive it since it makes a certain kind of impression, kind of like dressing for the job you want. Oh, and I almost forgot to say: the thoughtful young missionary who has been staying with us for the last month rode in the minivan too.

I guess I should give the missionary a name. Let's call him Caleb. I know that name sounds a bit different, Abby, and that's because he really is pretty unique! Caleb is from Utah, a world away from our life of politics and appearances. He just finished high school and is traveling around the country, visiting different communities and spreading the word of God. Good Christian families like ours are putting him up, and we were lucky enough to be chosen as the host family for Caleb during his time in the District.

Right away, I liked Caleb.

He's as handsome a boy as I've ever seen—almost like

Jimmy Stewart has come back to life. I wish you could see his eyes, Abby—bedroom, I tell you! And he's unbelievably polite—in a way that East Coast boys never are anymore. But most importantly, I felt like I could tell him anything, Abby, and I mean *anything*. I say this even though he hasn't spent much time outside of Utah, and I'm not sure how much he understands about life in the big city. For a while, I secretly wished he might fall in love with our neighbor's daughter and move in next door, but I realize now that's one fantasy I'll have to give up.

But I'm getting ahead of myself. Let me get back to my original story.

Taylor wanted to drive alone in the Beamer, so Caleb rode with us in the minivan. He sat in the passenger seat, following along on the map and entertaining the kids with sugar-laden cookies and fantastical stories about life out West. (Even I gasped when he told us about a hat-shaped rock balanced on top of a tiny mountain. Can you imagine?!)

In all honesty, Caleb has been a Godsend. I must admit that I often feel overwhelmed by the kids. Don't get me wrong, Abby, I love them more than any other mother has ever loved her children, but sometimes they are just too much for one woman to handle. I'm sure you and all the other mothers out there will understand what I mean.

And, of course, Taylor is simply not around. He's too busy at work to be bothered with things like tummy time or potty-training or parent-teacher meetings at the Montessori school. So I couldn't help but enjoy having Caleb with us on the trip, especially since, before that weekend, he spent most of his time at the church. But for two whole days, I basically had him all to myself.

I didn't intend to spend so much time alone with Caleb, but after we arrived and ate lunch, Taylor said he had a headache and wanted to lie down. My mother is so wonderful with the kids that I barely have to do a thing to keep them happy when we visit, and almost as soon as we'd unpacked the minivan, she had them immersed in finger painting. There was red, green, and blue paint all over the kitchen table, but—bless her heart!—she had a smile on her face as wide as the horizon. My father had disappeared with his fishing rod as usual, so that left Caleb and me with nothing to do.

Well, I don't know about you, Abby, but I think that when the good Lord is kind enough to give you a day of glorious sunshine and a giant bay full of sparkling water, you should enjoy it! The only reasonable thing to do was to take Daddy's old Chris Craft out for a ride.

Caleb had never been on a boat before, and it took him a while to get his sea legs: he tumbled into me a few times, but I was no worse for the wear. To be honest, it was just nice to have some fun for a change, and after a little while, I all but forgot I was a twenty-nine-year-old mother of two. Caleb wanted to know all about what it was like to grow up in the nation's capital, and he really seemed to be listening when I told him about a little girl who liked to search for Easter eggs on the White House lawn and climb inside the space capsule at the Smithsonian. He didn't even seem shocked when I admitted to being a teenager who snuck into the 9:30 Club when she was fifteen and barely made the Metro home at midnight. And I found myself remembering what it was like to be young all over again: the giddiness, the freedom, the intensity. Caleb even looked me in the eye: something Taylor rarely does. I tell you, Abby, I felt alive for the first time in a long time.

We went swimming after a while, and before I knew it, the sun was on the other side of the water, threatening to retire for the night. We climbed back on board, and I drove home as fast as I could. I just knew Taylor would be worried.

But when we returned, Taylor barely glanced in my direction. He had set up camp in front of Daddy's flat screen: a beer in one hand, the remote in the other, my father by his side in a similar position. My mother, in the kitchen preparing dinner, looked exhausted. Her eyelids opened and closed the same way my daughter's do when she's trying to stay awake during one of Pastor Skip's longer sermons at church.

I lifted our son from her arms, and Caleb took over the cooking, gently guiding my mother to a nearby chair. For a moment, I felt guilty about leaving her alone all day but reassured myself with the realization that these things happened almost as rarely as Taylor and I make love.

Supper was quiet, and it wasn't long before everyone was in bed: the kids breathing as soft as angels in the room next to ours, and Taylor gasping for air the way he always does after he's had too much to drink. I put a cold compress on his head and a glass of ice water on the bedside table, but I couldn't find sleep—my stomach had been nervous all night, and I hadn't been able to eat a thing—so I tiptoed out the bedroom door and stepped onto the back patio to watch the fireflies buzzing in the night.

To my complete surprise, Caleb was there, smoking and taking in the starry sky. I should have felt uncomfortable being alone with another man so late, but instead I found his presence calming. And when he held out a cigarette to me, I surprised myself again by accepting—the first time I had done so since high school. Lord knows what I was thinking, Abby.

We didn't say much—Caleb and me—but I could tell something was transpiring between us: we were connecting. His eyes would light up when I dared to meet his gaze, and when he finally did reach for my hand, his skin felt warm in mine. He led me down to the pier, and I was surprised to see how beautiful the bay looked at night: the lights glimmered off the water like a candy-colored carnival at sea.

Inside the boat, Caleb pulled me to him, and for some reason I still can't understand, I didn't resist. The nicotine buzzed in my head, and I felt a formidable rush when Caleb put his mouth on mine.

After that, I don't remember anything. I swear, Abby, I don't. Everything else was a blank.

The world looked different the next morning: the sun was too bright, the kids too needy, my husband . . . well, I don't know what to say about him. Too nothing, I suppose. But he was gone before I could figure out what seemed wrong or at least not right, gone back to the District in a rush of excuses and goodbyes. I packed his bag for him and waved as he drove away like any good wife would, but truthfully, I was more worried about my own mixed-up feelings than his safe return.

We took the kids to church—Caleb, my parents, and I— where Caleb introduced himself and said a few words to the congregation. He was funny and passionate and real. Everyone adored him, and I felt proud: like he somehow belonged to me. The rest of the day passed in a whirlwind of activity— swimming and sunning, eating and playing. The kids were easy-to-please and content, and I felt some of their peace too. Before I knew it, our time at the bay was over, and we were back on the road home.

Taylor didn't return until late that night, and I didn't want to bother him when he did. After all, what could I say? Could I even consider telling him the truth? Would he understand if I tried to explain how lonely and neglected I'd been feeling? How it felt like he never even noticed me anymore?

This brings me to the point of my letter, Abby, and my question for you, which is this: What am I supposed to do now?

To tell you the truth, I think I already know the answer to my own silly question . . .

Caleb will be gone within the week, and everything will go back to the way it was before, back to normal. Taylor will work too much, and I will be left with my routine: cooking and shopping, cleaning and washing, taking care of my lovely children, the beautiful babes who give my life purpose. Of course, the kids will be simply devastated by Caleb's departure, but we will have no choice but to soldier on like good little worker bees. And Taylor—well, I figure what he doesn't know won't hurt him, right? It wouldn't be the first thing he didn't know about me, though admittedly it would be the only secret I've kept from him since we wed.

Besides, Abby, I don't want to try to rationalize the irrational. There's no explanation for what happened. It just did. Two bodies came together in the dark, and, as far as I can tell, it was nothing more than a purely physical attraction. A one-time indulgence that doesn't really amount to much when it comes right down to it. I mean, I can't have real feelings for Caleb, Abby. For god's sake, he's just eighteen! And I certainly would never leave Taylor—after all, how would Caleb support us? And, my God, what would people say? It might be different if he were older, more settled, but in truth Caleb has absolutely nothing to offer us.

When I think about it now, I have to believe it was probably just the cigarettes, the sunshine, the sea air.

It wasn't real, Abby. It was a dream.

And I don't need to overanalyze what happened or wonder where it came from or what it means because it *can't* mean anything, Abby. No, it simply cannot. And besides, I know who I am: Mrs. Taylor . . . Well, let's just say, Mrs. Taylor Smith. And all my encounter with Caleb means is that I am human. I have sinned like anybody else. As long as I accept Jesus as my personal savior, I know he will forgive me, and I will be happy once again.

Don't you agree, Abby?

Signed,
Confused in the Capital

To Sleep, Perchance to Dream

Luz was addicted to sleep. Well, actually, it was dreaming she was hooked on. All day at work she thought about the moment each night when she would close her eyes and enter the comfortable world of subterranean desire and unconscious brainplay. It was there, in her dreams, that Luz was able to be the person she was too afraid to be in real life. It didn't matter if it was a dream about falling in love or a nightmare about falling from the sky. No matter what she encountered, Luz embraced these moments away from reality.

She liked to dream so much, in fact, that she had begun to do things to make it easier to enter sleep. At first she started with the obvious techniques: a cup of warm milk before bedtime, some instrumental music on the clock radio. She had soon added reading in bed to her list of tricks. These maneuvers helped Luz relax and better prepare for her nocturnal adventures, but they didn't help her fall asleep any faster, which was her real goal. So Luz decided to take a more proactive approach and began doing research about the best ways to make herself more prone to sleep.

Valerian root was the method recommended by internet herbalists, and this arrangement worked for a few weeks until

Luz grew immune to its properties. During this time, Luz found herself drifting away within an hour of taking the large white oval pill. Normally, Luz went to bed around ten—she had to be at work by eight every morning—but the Valerian root allowed her to nod off around nine, giving her a full hour of extra dream time.

Luz quickly adjusted to this bonus and often lost track of time at work fantasizing about the longer nights ahead. It was at a time like this when her boss, Connie, caught Luz wandering into the more hospitable places of her mind.

"If I didn't know you better, I'd think you were in love," Connie remarked to a starry-eyed Luz.

"What do you mean by that?" Luz asked, snapping out of her meditation.

"I mean that you never go out, so I can't fathom when you would have the opportunity to find someone to fall in love with."

"I go out," Luz said, objecting to Connie's depiction of her with as much artificial vehemence as she could muster.

"You have never once gone to the office holiday thing. You didn't come to my Super Bowl party. You don't do anything."

"I don't like football."

"Do you think I like football? It's just a way to meet people, Luz." Connie sighed before she went on. "You shouldn't give up, Luz. It may be too late for me, but you still have time."

"Connie," Luz said, wishing she could say more. Connie's husband had left her five years before—right after they both hit forty and, from his point of view, just in time for him to find a new wife, one who wanted children. Luz wanted to be supportive whenever the subject of love came up with Connie, but at the same time, she had no idea what she was supposed to say or how she was supposed to act. And what if the wrong words came out? Where would that leave her then?

Connie was still smiling sadly, but then her cheerful expression suddenly changed to a more serious one. "Don't start getting dreamy on me, Luz," Connie snapped. "I'd replace you in a minute."

In truth, Luz was one of those employees whom every boss longed to find: she was dependable and efficient, and she had few distractions. She was, in reality, somewhat irreplaceable. That was why Connie had reluctantly dragged Luz along with her as she steadily ascended the corporate ladder.

Like Connie, Luz had studied accounting, but she had never filled out the paperwork to transfer to a four-year school after finishing her associate's degree at NOVA. She knew she should have applied to a bachelor's program, but graduation had come at an inopportune time, six weeks after her mother's death. Luz had been forced to get a job in order to keep up with the mortgage payments on the two-bedroom condo she and her mother had shared since her father had left eleven years before. Luz knew she didn't need two bedrooms, and she was well aware that she could put an ad in the paper listing the room for rent, but even now, six years later, it didn't feel like her mother had vacated the space. Luz had long ago redecorated her mother's room, adding a desk and a futon after Connie's first promotion, but the carpet still maintained her mother's scent, and sometimes when Luz passed the room in a rush, she was sure that, out of the corner of her eye, she could see the fragile frame of her mother hovering in the doorway.

So the room stayed empty, and Luz kept working for Connie.

I t was before the time of Valerian Root that Luz had her first dream about Heath, one of the other district managers on the ninth floor. Heath was young for a manager—just twenty-eight, only two years older than Luz—and Connie never hesitated to make disparaging remarks about his age. Luz had not paid much attention to Heath before the dream, though it wasn't unusual for him to stop by her desk, so much so she often wondered if he thought she'd betray some secret about Connie to help him get ahead. But Luz was usually too wrapped up in her own assignments to notice the comings and goings of her coworkers.

Unlike most people, Luz appreciated her job. Her office was in a brand new high rise, and from the ninth floor—where she and Connie had been for just over a year—she could see just the tiniest sliver of the silver-colored Potomac. This view afforded Luz the ability to focus her attention on the beauty outside when she grew tired of the cubicle walls of her office.

But after her first dream about Heath—yes, there had been others—the image of the river failed to soothe her in the same way it once did. Instead Luz's gaze often wandered to the image her mind had created of Heath lounging by the rooftop pool of her condo tower, wearing nothing but his briefs. Luz knew that in real life Heath would not look as sculpted as he did in her nighttime fantasy. She could tell from the tightness of his belt that he probably had a small layer of fat around his middle. But she found it enjoyable to imagine Heath's sweet green eyes and too long nose on top of the chiseled body created by her unconscious, and her response had been to will herself to dream more and stare out the window less. It wasn't long after that when Luz started in with the warm milk.

But soon the drink failed to serve its purpose, as did the Valerian root, and Luz ended up perusing the shelves at the Wal-Drug on the first floor of her office building for a more potent elixir.

Connie found Luz in the sleep-aide aisle, and Luz felt herself blush. Would Connie suspect why Luz longed for sleep?

"Do you really have trouble sleeping, Luz?" Connie asked. "Lately you seem so refreshed."

Luz hesitated before responding. She wasn't sure how much she should share with Connie, if she could trust her. "Well, actually, I *have* been sleeping very well these days. And I do feel better."

"Really?" Connie sounded exasperated, and Luz tried to remember the last time Connie had been interested in anything she said. "You have to tell me your secret. I've got bags under my eyes that look like elephant skin. You'd think I was ten years older than I am."

Luz had noticed the circles under Connie's eyes. As well as the wrinkles sprouting from her mouth like weeds. But Luz would never admit this to Connie, so instead she told her about the Valerian root. "It's in aisle Six-A. With the vitamins," she said.

"Isn't that the same stuff they put in Sleepytime Tea?"

Connie asked, but Luz didn't know the answer, and she was so intrigued by the idea of tea that made you sleepy that she found herself making excuses to get away from Connie so she could search for the potion herself.

Connie was right. The main ingredient in Sleepytime Tea was Valerian root. Luz was so incredibly disappointed with this news that by the time she got home she had decided to drown her sorrows in a big cup of tea and two of the magic white pills. Sleep came easier and more quickly that night than it had in as long as Luz could remember, and in her dreams, she was a cowgirl: riding on the back of a spotted horse across Rock Creek Park, an unknown man in a ten-gallon hat in front of her confidently holding the reins.

Doubling up on Valerian root, or tripling up as it were, only worked for a few meager days. Then Luz started to feel anxious and moody; she still didn't have a solution to her problem. Back at Wal-Drug, the pharmacist directed her to the sleeping pills. Luz took her purchase home and read the directions. The bottle said to take one blue pill before bedtime, and she decided to obey the rules.

At least for the time being.

She was pleased to find that the new pill had an even more pronounced effect than the Valerian root. After taking it, she struggled to keep her eyes open for a mere fifteen minutes. Soon the little blue pills became a regular part of Luz's life. She made a habit of taking them while she ate her dinner, so she would fall asleep as soon as she finished. The only problem was the sleeping pills made her so drowsy that it became difficult to wake the next morning. The alarm would go off at six, and Luz would feel groggy and disoriented. She'd play a game of tag with the clock radio, letting the snooze wake her every nine minutes until she could no longer put off the inevitable. Eventually, the problem carried over to her job. Luz was late only three times before Connie said something.

"I've never known you to be late before, Luz. You're usually the epitome of punctual."

"I'm sorry," Luz mumbled without looking up.

"Luz," Connie started, and she waited until she caught Luz's eye to continue. "Luz, is there something wrong?"

Luz thought she saw a trace of concern in her boss's face, but she just couldn't be sure.

"Do you want to talk about it?" Connie asked. "We could take a long lunch, catch up on each other's lives."

Luz thought it was odd that Connie suggested they "catch up" since, from Luz's point of view, the two of them knew only the most cursory things about each other. "Catch up" meant filling each other in on the events of the past few weeks. In reality, the two of them would have years to cover before they would be caught up, years of sorrow and loss, disappointment and regret. So rather than consider Connie's invitation, Luz avoided it altogether. "I guess I'm just having trouble sleeping," she offered.

"Are you still taking that Valerian root? I tried it for a few days, but that stuff can be addicting."

Luz studied Connie's face, contemplating what she should say before she answered. "No, I don't take that anymore. I'm probably just having trouble getting used to sleeping without it." Then Luz busied herself with rearranging the items on her desk.

Connie paused before she replied, and Luz could feel her boss's eyes on her. "Well, good," she finally said. "I'm glad you're not relying on pills to get you through the night."

Luz jerked her head up when Connie said this. "I'm fine," she said defensively.

"Are you sure? You could take some time off or something. You've probably accumulated enough time to go away for weeks. I can't remember the last time you took a personal day."

Nothing scared Luz more than the idea of a vacation. What would she do with herself for a whole seven days? She could barely make it through a single weekend alone, much less an entire week. "No, I'll be okay. Really. I'll rest up tonight."

L uz was determined to make good on her promise to Connie so that night she ate a big dinner: turkey with all the trimmings. She knew from her internet research that the tryptophan in turkey was supposed to put people to sleep. Before her mother had died, the two of them often cooked together all weekend, making casseroles and cookies to share with the residents of the halfway house around the corner. But there was no time to prepare so much food on a weeknight, so Luz hit the frozen food aisle of her grocery store and bought two turkey dinners and an apple pie. She set up a TV tray in the living room so she could watch an hour of *Everybody Loves Raymond* reruns while she ate. She swallowed two blue pills with her meal—just to be safe—and nodded off before the last scene had finished.

While she slept, Luz dreamed about the tall man who played Raymond's brother on the TV show: Brad Garrett. In her dream, Garrett was working as a security officer in the lobby of her building. When she saw him standing there, Luz smiled flirtatiously in his direction. He smiled back at her and said, "Hello, beautiful," his deep voice echoing off the marble walls like thunder. Then Luz went up and put her arms around his neck so that he would know she wanted him to lean down and kiss her. They were still lip-locked when Luz woke up and found herself sprawled out on the sofa, the television remote between her legs and her dirty napkin on her stomach.

Luz managed to make it to work on time that day and every day for the next two weeks. She got around her snooze problem by moving the alarm clock to the other side of the room and cranking it to the maximum volume. Even on the days when she was desperate to pull the covers over her head and ignore the loud beeping, she convinced herself to get up so she wouldn't have to deal with another interrogation from Connie.

In the meantime, Connie's generosity had run out. There were no more offers of vacations, no more sympathetic chats. Instead Connie had Luz working overtime and doing things that were not even part of her job description. Luz was used to this kind of behavior from Connie, who acted that way every time she had an approaching deadline.

"Luz!" Connie yelled from her windowed office one morning. "Did you pick up the portfolios from marketing yet?

They said they'd be ready at ten."

Luz was about to say she was on her way when Heath walked up and spoke for her. "It's only nine-forty, Connie. For God's sake, why don't you just chill?" Heath put his arm on Luz's cubicle wall and leaned toward her like they were old friends.

Luz had seen Heath act that way with other women in the office, figured he did it with all of them, so it always made her nervous when he stopped at her desk.

And then, to make matters worse, he turned in her direction and spoke directly to her: "You look different, Luz." When she felt her mouth drop open, his face turned red, but he went on. "I don't mean to embarrass you or anything. I just thought maybe you'd been working out or something."

Luz was stunned. She wasn't even aware Heath knew her name, much less what she looked like. She was also shocked that someone as high up as Heath had noticed how much her body had changed over the past few weeks. Luz had always been too thin—she had the kind of figure people so often compared to sticks or birds—but ever since she'd been taking the sleeping pills, her curves had begun to fill out, as if the little blue pills were hormonal rather than narcotic.

"Have you ever tried that bike path along the Potomac?" Heath asked, and Luz realized he had been rambling on the whole time.

"Leave her alone, Thompson," Connie said, as she walked up to Heath and knocked his elbow off Luz's cubicle wall. "She's all mine," Connie said and turned to walk away.

Luz wasn't sure what Connie meant by that, but she was

more concerned with Heath than Connie at that moment. When she looked back at him, Heath spoke to her in a whisper: "Deadline, huh? It's even worse than when she's P.M.S.-ing. Well, I've got to bolt. Catch you later, L.B."

Heath was gone before Luz had a chance to ask how he knew her middle initial. She watched him move past the other cubicles without stopping at anyone else's desk, and after he got on the elevator, she absentmindedly wrote out her name on the piece of paper in front of her: Luz Beverly Martinez.

That night, Luz waited until after she had turned off the television to take her pills. She retired to her bedroom, where she put on her favorite nightgown: the purple one with the white polka dots. She lit the candle next to her bed and got under the covers. Once she felt comfortable, she reached over for the glass of water she had put on the bedside table and took three blue pills. Then she closed her eyes and willed herself to think of Heath. She was determined to dream about him that night. It took a little longer than normal, but when she finally drifted off, Heath was there, waiting for her like a unshakeable suitor. This time it was Heath who was dressed up like a security guard. Only he wasn't working at their building. He was standing outside the gym Luz passed every day after she got off the Metro and walked the two blocks to her condo in Crystal City.

"Hey, L.B.," he said. "You look nice."

Luz blushed and shuffled by without saying anything, but after she turned the corner, she had a change of heart and walked back to the gym. Heath was still there, and when she approached, he said the exact same thing: "Hey, L.B. You look nice."

She stopped and stared at him. Was he making fun of her? But after a moment he said it again: "Hey, L.B. You look nice." She couldn't believe how rude he was being. She was about to leave when he said it again. She stood there for another moment and waited to see if he would repeat himself, and he did. He said it over and over until finally Luz couldn't stand it anymore, and she turned and sprinted all the way home even though, by then, she had lost her shoes and had to run barefoot.

After that dream, Luz stopped watching the show with Brad Garrett. Something about seeing Heath in uniform had ruined it for her. She switched to *Felicity*, the show about the girl who follows a boy to college. She also avoided Heath at work. The last dream had felt so real, so intimate, that she worried it would be uncomfortable to see him again. But she needn't have worried. Heath didn't show his face around her desk for a week. She told herself it was for the best, especially since Connie was becoming more and more demanding every day. She had Luz picking up her dry cleaning and doing her grocery shopping. One afternoon, she even asked Luz to stop by her apartment in Bethesda and feed her cats on the way home.

"But I live in Virginia," Luz pointed out.

Connie laughed out loud, but Luz had no idea what was funny. "Listen, Luz, if there's a problem, by all means, just say so. I mean, the cats will probably starve, but that's fine.

"There's no problem. It's just *not* on my way home. You said to *stop by on my way home*."

"Good God, Luz, I *was* kidding!" Connie snorted. "Sometimes you scare me. In fact, why don't you go home early? You look beat."

L uz had taken to eating big meals at night ever since the turkey dinner. In fact, she tried to eat as little as possible all day, so she could stuff herself in the evenings. She found that the more she ate for dinner, the easier it was to fall asleep. She had even dragged her mattress into the living room so she could eat in front of the television and then drift off to sleep without interruption. She usually did the dishes the next morning before she went to work.

That night, Luz decided to stop at the Chinese place next to the gym for lo mein and dumplings. Eating noodles always made her lethargic and content. Her good dreams now alternated between Heath and the two young college boys on the *Felicity* show. Brad Garrett even made a return appearance every now and then. At the same time, the bad dreams had taken a surprising turn: her mother, as familiar to her as any celebrity, was now starring in Luz's own personal home movies. But most nights, Luz's mother hid in dark corners or under shadowy eaves, never allowing Luz to get a good look at her.

I t wasn't long after that when Luz started waking up during the night. Sometimes she would have to go to the bathroom, her bladder screaming at her like a sick child. And other times she simply found she could no longer sleep. She had been taking three of the little blue pills ever since the day Heath stopped at her desk, and she was afraid to increase the dosage further since the directions said not to exceed one pill every twenty-four hours. Often she would fall back asleep, only to wake up late—despite her blaring alarm clock. On days like these, she skipped her shower to save time. She'd zip herself into a skirt, throw on her jacket and head out the door without so much as a look in the mirror. At work, she'd brush her hair and apply her makeup in the bathroom mirror, avoiding Connie as much as possible until after she had put herself together.

During one of those rushed mornings, she ran into Heath in the lobby of the building. At first, she wasn't even sure he recognized her since it took him a moment to speak, his mouth as wide as an open door.

"Wow, Luz, you look—" Heath stopped without finishing. "You look . . . well, I guess you had a wild night, huh?" He pointed to her unkempt hair, and Luz tried to smooth it back into place in the mirrored elevator doors. "No, really," Heath said. "It's a good look for you. I just never knew you were like that. I always took you for the type who likes to stay at home and nest."

"You did?" Luz asked politely though in truth she felt gutted: she could sense her jaw beginning to shake and the tears developing behind her eyes. She focused her attention on the LED light that flashed the floor numbers as the elevator made its way down and hoped Heath would leave her alone. When the elevator finally arrived, she stepped in without looking back, but Heath followed her anyway.

"I didn't hurt your feelings, did I?" Heath said after they were alone in the elevator. "Geez, I didn't mean it like that. I can nest with the best of them. God, I'm sorry. I'm such a loser."

This made Luz laugh.

"It's nice when you smile, Luz," Heath said. "You have a great smile."

Luz's cheeks burned. She couldn't imagine what would happen next.

"I hate to think I've upset you, Luz. I mean, I know about your mother and all. It must have been really difficult."

Luz was completely taken aback. Even though she had her mother's picture on her desk, no one ever asked about it. Not even Connie. It was as if her mother had never existed. "How did you know my middle name was Beverly?" Luz demanded.

"I didn't. I just saw your name on a file once: Luz B. Martinez."

"And you remembered that?"

"Of course, Luz. You're kind of hard to forget, you know?"

Luz felt her face grow completely red. She wanted to look away but instead let herself turn her head slightly in his direction. "You're not a loser," she said.

"No, I am. I *really* am. I mean, look." He turned in her direction and pointed at her. "I've gone and upset you. I hate that. I mean, you must know I like you."

Luz was too embarrassed to look at Heath, so she watched his wavy reflection in the doors of the elevator. His image was distorted, stretched out like it would be in a funhouse mirror, and she let out a giggle before she knew what was happening.

"Do you want to go to happy hour with me tonight?" Heath asked her. "It doesn't have to be a real date or anything. A few people from the office are going. Who knows? It might be fun. Even with a loser like me."

Luz was too stunned to respond, but Heath pressed her.

"Well?" he said. "What do you think?"

"Okay." And then: "I guess so."

"Great. Meet me in the lobby at six, and we'll walk over together."

Before Luz could reconsider, the elevator doors opened on the seventh floor, the marketing department, and Heath was gone.

L uz dreamed all day about her plans with Heath. She thought about how she'd sit, what she'd order to drink, the way Heath would lean in closer and closer as the night went on. She even bought a new scent at Wal-Drug during her lunch break. She wanted everything to be perfect, and not even Connie's impositions could snap Luz out of her reverie.

"What's with you, Luz?" Connie asked late in the day. "You seem downright giddy."

Luz felt shy, but she also wanted to share her good news with someone. "I'm going out," she said excitedly.

"Wow, good for you, Luz," Connie said. "Really, I'm happy for you." Connie smiled but her eyes betrayed a sadness Luz had seen there many times before.

A t five-thirty, Luz went to the bathroom to touch up her makeup and adjust her clothes. By quarter till six, she was ready. She decided that in situations like these, it was always best to be prompt, so she made her way to the elevator and arrived in the lobby a few minutes early. As soon as her Timex flashed a six and two zeroes, Luz trained her focus on the elevator doors, expecting Heath to arrive exactly on time.

After the elevator had unloaded a handful of people, Luz looked at her wrist again, realizing she was foolish to expect Heath to be there right at six. Not everyone was as reliable as she was. Nevertheless, the slightest bit of doubt crept into Luz's brain, and she decided to step outside so that no one from the office would see her waiting if Heath decided not to show. She knew that once they got off the elevator, most people took the back hallway to the parking garage and that she could still see the elevator from her position outside the building's glass front.

It wasn't long before Luz watched Connie get off the elevator. Afraid of being spotted, Luz stepped back from the entryway. But Connie had her head in her purse as she walked in the direction of the garage, and she never noticed Luz's eyes on her. The elevator doors opened again a minute later, and this time it was Heath who appeared. He looked around the lobby but didn't see Luz peering through the front window. Luz told herself to open the door and go inside, but no matter how hard she tried, her body resisted her instructions. Instead, she stood there, just watching him. Even though he was facing away from her, she could see in the mirrored doors of the elevator that he had taken off his tie and unbuttoned his shirt. His usually smooth face was defined by an unfamiliar dark stubble, adding a shade of distinction to his big nose.

He looked beautiful to Luz. Simply perfect.

In that moment, Luz understood that things would never be this good between them again. And as soon as she realized this, Heath spun around in a semicircle and looked directly at her, as if he too could hear her thoughts. He smiled and waved in her direction, but Luz backed away from the building without responding. Then she turned from the building and ran all the way to her regular Metro stop.

On the train ride home, Luz planned her evening. She'd stop at the store and buy her dinner. It would have to be something easy because *Felicity* started at seven. Frozen pizza perhaps. She'd eat her pizza and take her pills: three blue pills and one white, a new prescription. She'd swallow them with her warm milk and watch as Felicity would do things that seemed absolutely impossible to Luz. And then Luz would return to the world of her dreams, the world where she too could do whatever she wanted.

The Season for Giving

DATE: Wed, 27 Oct 2010 16:29:33 (EST)

FROM: "Dr. Caroline Baker-Gallant"
          <bakerc@johnshopkins.edu>

SUBJECT: Thanksgiving menu

TO: "Mom" <RetiredinFlorida@yahoo.com>,
          "Justine" <JustineJennaJulieJoe@hotmail.com>

Dear Mom and Justine,

   It looks like Teddy and I will be able to come to Justine and Joe's house in Indianapolis for Thanksgiving after all. (I can't wait to see little Jenna and Julie again! It's been way too long since the time we tried—unsuccessfully, I might add— to take them to the aquarium here. By the way, have they gotten over their unusual fear of fish yet?) Teddy and I will fly in Wednesday morning and leave on Saturday.

   Justine and I decided on the phone last night that it would be helpful to put together a Thanksgiving menu. (We don't want another Thanksgiving fiasco because we tried to do too much—remember the time in Florida when Mom walked out, and we had to eat tuna out of the can?!) There are ten items on the list, so if each of the five of us (Caroline & Teddy, Justine & Joe, and then Mom, of course) makes two dishes, that would be perfect. Dividing the labor this way will mean that no one person will be overworked, and the boys can contribute equally for a change.

Mom makes the best stuffing, and Justine does a super sweet potato casserole, so those choices are obvious. I baked Parker House rolls last Thanksgiving with Teddy's family in Boston, and they were fabulous (if I do say so myself), so I would be happy to prepare those again. (Even though it is quite labor intensive, it's good for me to stay away from knives—after all, my surgeon's hands are insured!) I've included the menu below and made suggestions about who can make what (Justine has a to-die-for cranberry salad recipe from Aunt Kay, so I put her down for that), but, really, I am *totally* flexible about who makes what (though I don't want to change the menu at this late date). The only thing I don't know how to prepare is apple pie. Mom—do you have a good recipe?

If you both tell me which items you would like to make (Justine: please let me know about Joe too), I'll make a final to-do list based on your requests. By the way, if it sounds appealing, we can add the mouth-watering spinach salad (with sugar-coated pecans) that Teddy's sister made last Thanksgiving. She took a culinary course at the Sorbonne, and she's the absolute best cook I have ever known!

As for Jenna and Julie, they can be in charge of the vanilla ice cream and the drinks if you want to include them, Justine. It's up to you. (I don't know if they're old enough for that since I'm not a Mommy yet, but they have to be more grown up than they were when they peed on my Pottery Barn sofa!) (Speaking of being a Mommy, we're implanting seven embryos in December! Can you believe it?! Friends of ours had triplets this way last spring—it was an Easter miracle! But don't tell Aunt Mary yet. I don't want her asking if I can still conceive. She'll never let me forget about my "operation" in college, will she?) What about punch? Wouldn't that be fun? I usually mix 7-Up with O.J. or pineapple juice—maybe the girls are finally mature enough to handle that.

Let me know what you want to make as soon as you have the chance!

Best,
Caroline

THANKSGIVING MENU

Turkey and Gravy—Teddy

Green Bean Casserole—Joe or Teddy

Stuffing—Mom

Sweet Potato Casserole—Justine

Mashed Potatoes—Mom or Teddy

Broccoli Casserole—Joe or Teddy

Cranberry Salad—Justine

Apple Pie (my favorite!)—?????

Parker House Rolls—Caroline

Pumpkin Pie—Caroline

DATE: Thur, 28 Oct 2010 07:18:47 (CST)

FROM: "Justine, Jenna, Julie & Joe Hall"
          <JustineJennaJulieJoe@hotmail.com>

SUBJECT: Re: Thanksgiving Menu

TO: "Caroline" <bakerc@johnshopkins.edu>,
          "Mom" <RetiredinFlorida@yahoo.com>

I'll do the sweet potato casserole, the green bean casserole, and the cranberry sauce. Is that all right with you, Caroline? I can also make the mashed potatoes if need be. As for the girls, all I care about is that they don't have anything with caffeine, sugar, or preservatives. (We wouldn't want them to have a sugar rush!) A nearby grocery store (actually it's a farmer's market owned and operated by my yoga teacher) has the most amazing organic, sugar-free pies: the strawberry, rhubarb, and blueberry are the best. Joe's parents buy a dozen pies every time they visit. (Pies make excellent gifts!) I don't know if you're opposed to serving something store-bought, Caroline (because I know how particular you are!), but it's definitely better than anything I could ever make and always, always fresh. (Besides, we like to keep things simple here. You know, "go with the flow" is what Joe always says.) Food for thought. Gotta run—the girls are fighting.

Love ya,
Justine

DATE: Thur, 28 Oct 2010 10:57:07 (EST)

FROM: "Dr. Caroline Baker-Gallant"
<bakerc@johnshopkins.edu>

SUBJECT: Re: Re: Thanksgiving menu

TO: "Justine" <JustineJennaJulieJoe@hotmail.com>,
"Mom" <RetiredinFlorida@yahoo.com>

You only have to make two things, Justine, not three! I'll put you down for the sweet potatoes and the cranberry salad. By the way, Aunt Kay's recipe is for cranberry salad, *not* cranberry sauce. (Don't worry, lots of people make that mistake!) I think the cranberry salad is a little harder to get right, and since you've done it successfully before, you'll know what you're doing. Let me know what Joe wants to make when he gets back from Memphis, or I can email him directly if that's easier—just send me his email address at work. (For some reason, I never got it the last time I asked for it.)

The local pies sound great. We can buy an apple pie and one other pie if you'd like. Blueberry or pecan sounds best to me—what do you all like?—but I would rather make the pumpkin pie. It only takes a few minutes, and Teddy loves my recipe. Oh, and don't forget the vanilla ice cream. There's no point in having pie without ice cream! (I'm sure the girls will want their pie a la mode too!)

Thanks for being Thanksgiving central, Justine! I appreciate you accommodating us!

Best,
Caroline

DATE: Fri, 29 Oct 2010 18:46:28 (EST)

FROM: "Barbie Baker" <RetiredinFlorida@yahoo.com>

SUBJECT: Re: Re: Re: Thanksgiving Menu—Mom's Response
            to Thanksgiving

TO: "Justine" <JustineJennaJulieJoe@hotmail.com>,
            "Caroline" <bakerc@johnshopkins.edu>

Dear girls,

Let's cut the broccoli casserole from the menu (it's full of
fat) and substitute the spinach salad that Caroline mentioned.
I also don't mind having baked sweet potatoes instead of the
sweet potato casserole with all the sugar. We can even replace
the green bean casserole with French green beans with
almonds (less calories than the casserole). Just use frozen
packages because it's easier. Gravy can be made by adding the
turkey drippings and some of the dark meat to a jar of store-
bought turkey gravy. This is simpler at the last minute when
the kitchen is busy.

I agree that the boys should contribute equally, so I have
assigned them the job of cooking and carving the turkey. (See
my revised menu below.)

Remember that whenever you have a big dinner like this,
it's a three-day process. We'll need to do the shopping on
Tuesday. Then I would like to make the stuffing after breakfast
on Wednesday. It can be cooked in the oven and refrigerated.
I will put it in two nine-by-thirteen glass pans. That way it can
be warmed in the microwave on Friday for leftovers and on
Thursday while the turkey is in the oven. The rolls should be

put in as soon as the turkey comes out and begins to cool (before carving). Also, if we use boxed mashed potatoes instead of making them from scratch, those can also be made at the last minute. The carver should begin slicing the turkey before everyone sits down to dinner and while drinks are being served. Gravy must be heated up at this time as well. Baked sweet potatoes will come out of the oven with the turkey, and they will hold their heat for thirty minutes until dinner if wrapped in a double kitchen towel on a serving platter.

I am all for buying the desserts: the rhubarb and pumpkin pies. The bakery near Justine's house sounds perfect. I will buy them if Justine places the order and plans to pick them up Thursday morning. I suggest that the children have the duty of setting the table (with supervision, of course). I would like to do this with them on Thursday afternoon. Do we want iced tea or water with dinner? I will be glad to make iced tea on Wednesday if you would like. The children can help pour the drinks and fill the glasses with ice when the turkey comes out of the oven. If we follow the itinerary I've laid out below, everything should go as planned and make for a perfectly pleasant holiday.

Love and miss you,
Mom

REVISED THANKSGIVING MENU

Cook, carve, and platter the turkey—Joseph and Ted
Right before dinner on Thursday

Cranberry salad—Justine
Wednesday after lunch

(*Do we have a recipe for this?*)
(*On second thought, we can just use canned cranberry sauce.*)

Frozen French green beans with almonds—Justine
After turkey goes in the oven on Thursday

Spinach salad—Caroline
Wednesday after lunch

Homemade rolls—Caroline
Make on Thursday after breakfast? Or Wednesday?

Mashed potatoes—Justine
Right before dinner on Thursday

Iced tea—Mom & Ted
Wednesday after lunch

Baked sweet potatoes—Caroline
Wash and prepare on Wednesday
(cook in oven with turkey)

Stuffing—Mom
Wednesday after lunch

Gravy—Mom
Again, after turkey goes in the oven

Set Table—Joseph and Justine
Thursday afternoon with Jenna and Julie

Ice in glasses before dinner—Justine, Mom, and the girls
Right before dinner

Cut and serve pies after dinner—Ted
Caroline will dish out ice cream

Clear dishes from table—Caroline

Scrape, rinse and stack dishes—Mom

Load dishes in dishwasher—Justine

Put leftovers in the refrigerator—Caroline

Finish carving the turkey and put it in the refrigerator for
leftovers—Joseph

DATE: Fri, 29 Oct 2010 19:48:42 (CST)

FROM: "Justine, Jenna, Julie & Joe Hall"
<JustineJennaJulieJoe@hotmail.com>

SUBJECT: Re: Re: Re: Re: Thanksgiving Menu—Mom's
Response to Thanksgiving

TO: "Caroline" <bakerc@johnshopkins.edu>

Oh, Caroline!

I don't have much time to write—totally lost track of time
scrapbooking this afternoon and wait until you see the
gorgeous page I created for Jenna's birthday book!—but I want
to tell you that I'm not sure what's going on with Mom or why
she has created this elaborate protocol. I swear I had nothing
to do with any of it! Promise you won't blame me???

Just don't think about it too much, Caroline. (I know how
much you like to over-think things!) You and I will make sure
that Thanksgiving will be relaxing and enjoyable despite
Mom's attempts to control every calorie that goes in our
mouths. I mean, it's not like you have to worry about your

weight anymore—you'll be eating for two soon. Or maybe even eight!

What I can't figure about Mom is why she doesn't understand that we don't have to plan everything out in advance anymore. Thank God we're so laid back and didn't inherit her desire to micro-manage. Can you believe how times have changed?! Please don't worry about her absolutely ridiculous plan. Just stay calm, and I promise to take care of everything, okay?

Gotta run—Joe's on his way home, and you know how he likes to eat right at six. If I don't get on the stick, I'll never get the girls down by their bedtime!

XOXO,

Justine

P.S. You said blueberry and rhubarb, right?

Night Five

Until the summer of my twelfth year, I spent a good percentage of my time fantasizing about going to sleepaway camp. As long as I could remember, I had wanted desperately to take part in the sleeping-bag-and-s'mores ritual that so many other kids talked about. All of my neighbors went to camp, but I had not yet had the chance. I was the only one on our street who went to Catholic school, and camp wasn't something Catholic school kids did—maybe because in New Jersey the Catholics never had as much money as the Jews or maybe because Catholic parents, who prided themselves on repressing adolescent sexuality, knew what really went on at sleepaway camp. The latter was my secret hope, and I prided myself on knowing everything there was to know about late-night pranks and makeout sessions. In case I ever got the chance to go to camp, I wanted to be prepared.

Most of my knowledge about summer camp came from books—I was an avid reader of young adult fiction. I had studied every Judy Blume and Beverly Cleary book ever written and had long been romanced by the idea of a week spent in the mountains, far away from home and parents. I had devoured scene after scene in books with names like *Forever* and *There's a Bat in Bunk Five* and daydreamed about leisurely days spent lolling about in the soft, warm waters of never-ending blue-green lakes (lakes that made the reservoir where my mother took my sister and me on day trips every summer look like muddy bathwater). I longed to sit around a blazing campfire and eat a perfectly burnt marshmallow under the stars or snuggle inside a down-lined sleeping bag with a mysterious boy from Philadelphia or even just nearby Trenton. So when Debby D'Angelo, who lived five houses down from us and went to public school even though she too was Catholic, asked if I wanted to go to Hidden Valley with her the summer after sixth grade, I didn't hesitate.

After some cajoling, my parents finally acquiesced. They didn't have any objection to sleepaway camp (or so they said)—it just wasn't something they had ever considered an option. Now, years later, I can look back and understand that sleepaway camp was often a place people sent their kids because they didn't want to deal with them, but when I was young it never occurred to me that summer camp could hold its own appeal for parents. My own parents balked when they found out that Hidden Valley cost just over three hundred dollars, more than half of what they paid to send me to Immaculate Conception each year. I countered by explaining that my grade school didn't provide food or lodging, and they wrote the checks—four installments in April, May, June and the last on the day of my departure date on the first of July—without further complaint.

Technically, Hidden Valley was a Girl Scout camp, but just next door to the girls' camp was Blue Bear, the companion Boy

Scout camp. The brochure advertised numerous co-ed activities and even a dance the last night of the week. In my dreams, I imagined moonlit walks along the lake and first kisses under the stars.

The trip started to veer off the path of my carefully constructed fantasy while we were still making the four-hour trip from suburban New Jersey to rural Pennsylvania.

Everything had gone well during my initial departure. The bus—a sleek silver charter with seats that reclined and little ashtrays in the armrests—loomed large and promised more good things to come. Minutes later the bus pulled away from the crowd of devoted station wagons clustered together on the blacktop, and as Debby and I waved to our parents through the tinted bus windows, I began to sense the feeling of dread that would stay with me for the next seven days and nights.

Debby's father had to work that day—my mother often complained about how much time he spent at the office, especially on weekends—and Debby's mother, in a tank top and jeans, looked tired and disheveled, probably from having to care for their five kids by herself most of the time. My own mother was dressed in her Sunday best. She wore a sleeveless floral number that wrapped around her body like a sarong and tied at the waist. She waved perfectly, her arm rotating back and forth with precision, a middle-class princess. My father had his hand on her shoulder, his Rutgers t-shirt inching up his arm and revealing the clear line of a farmer's tan, even though he was a regional sales rep for Travelers Insurance. Dad waved more frantically than my mother, as if worried about my safe return. Even then, I knew that losing me was his greatest fear. Something in the way they watched me as the bus pulled away made me suddenly aware of my mistake: I was leaving behind the only people in the world who loved me without reservation.

Nevertheless, I tried to ignore the sudden apprehension I felt, so I could concentrate on the good things ahead. Debby and I didn't have much to talk about during the four-hour ride to Pennsylvania. We already knew everything about each other. I knew that Debby was smart and got good grades in school even though she never talked about it with anyone else and pretended not to know anything around boys, I knew she kept her hair shoulder-length because she didn't want it to be long like every other girl we knew, I knew she had been irritated with me in the spring when I got the same ten-speed she had picked out for her thirteenth birthday, and I knew that—even though it was a sin—Debby's mother had had her tubes tied so she wouldn't get pregnant again after Debbie's little brother, the D'Angelo's fifth, was born the previous summer.

And she knew just as much about me.

She knew that I loved to show off my smarts and entered every math and spelling bee in central Jersey, she knew that I hated my shoulder-length hair and couldn't wait until my mother would let me grow it out when I started high school, she knew that for some reason unknown to both of us I told my mother everything, and that I was also still afraid to sleep in my room alone at night.

What else was there besides that?

We were both good at almost everything we tried—

swimming, roller skating, sunbathing, biking, basketball, skateboarding, softball—but Debby seemed to gain confidence from her skills, whereas I somehow managed to find mine lacking. I also knew that even though she was only a year ahead of me in school, Debby had already had a boy's hand inside her pants, that she'd gotten drunk on several occasions and smoked pot just once. I, on the other hand, had barely tasted beer and hadn't even been kissed. And I feared that this was the unavoidable fate of a good Catholic schoolgirl.

We were about halfway to our destination when our bus—like the engine that couldn't—finally gave out on a hill near the top of a particularly steep Allegheny mountain. Luckily—or so we were told—this happened all the time. In half an hour, the engine would cool, and we could resume our trip west. The unlucky part, the part the two counselors on the bus neglected to tell us but which became readily apparent once we started moving again, was that we could no longer use the air conditioning.

"I can't believe how hot it is," I said to Debby as we cruised past the dilapidated shanties and deserted gas stations that dotted the Pennsylvania landscape.

"Oh, it'll be even hotter when we get there." Debby said this as if it would somehow alleviate the oppressiveness of the present heat, but instead the effect was alarming.

"What do you mean 'it will be hotter,'" I asked. "Isn't there any air conditioning?"

Debby scoffed: "Of course not, stupid."

It might have offended some people to be called "stupid," but I knew it was just Debby's way and a big reason why our friendship worked: she liked being in charge, she liked knowing more than me.

"No air conditioning?" I asked again. "Are you serious?"

"Trust me, you'll survive. You made it through nine months of confirmation training. I think you can handle this."

It had never even occurred to me that there wouldn't be any air conditioning at Hidden Valley. And why would it? I had never been anywhere before in my entire life without air-conditioning, at least not that I could I remember. The idea that I would have to go seven whole days without air conditioning was nearly as frightening as the idea of getting left behind on a school field trip or being held underwater by one of the older kids at the neighborhood pool. Already, I felt stifled by the thick air inside the bus. I leaned toward the open window, desperate to catch a breeze, but my forehead and the back of my neck had begun to sweat and my hair was sticking to my skin as if it had been zapped with static.

I couldn't imagine what I would do if the trip got any worse, so I did the only thing I knew how to do in times of crisis: I prayed, just like I had prayed for snow and the requisite snow day so many winters before. Only that day I prayed for a different kind of cold: air conditioning. In the time it took to drive the rest of the way to Hidden Valley, I recited two and a half rosaries in my head. I knew I couldn't do so without moving my lips, but I didn't care if Debby suspected me of believing in the power of prayer.

To my surprise, my faith delivered. The dining hall at Hidden Valley was air-conditioned. And to my relief, upon arrival we were shepherded there for our first camp-wide meeting. That is, after we had unloaded our sleeping bags and backpacks into the small, feeble shelters that they called cabins—which weren't really cabins, but slabs of cement block surrounded on all five sides with canvas tent flaps we had to unroll to protect ourselves from the elements.

"This is it?" I asked Debby in an exasperated tone when I saw the prison-like conditions of our accommodations.

"What did you expect?" Debby said, clearly put off by my response. "Shangri-La? It isn't called 'camping out' for nothing."

Back at the dining hall, the camp's head counselor, Coach Heidi, a fit woman with bowling ball breasts that seemed completely out of proportion with the rest of her tight frame, led us through an involved introduction to everything Hidden Valley.

Debby snorted when Coach Heidi folder her arms across her chest, an unsuccessful attempt to conceal her ample upper half. "Hide me, Heidi!" she said with a laugh.

Despite her well-endowed bosom and her relatively young age—I figured she looked to be in her late thirties—Heidi appeared frail, as if approaching an early death. I couldn't help but wonder why someone so weak looking would have wanted to assume such an active position, but when Coach Heidi spoke, her voice contradicted her appearance: she sounded more fortified than any woman I had ever met before, as if she had the energy and resolution of twenty men. From her spot in front of the massive stone fireplace, Coach Heidi stood above the few hundred Girl Scouts seated on the floor around her and shouted out each and every camp rule as if they were instructions for nuclear fallout: "NO snacking between meals. NO smoking. You MUST wear shower shoes in the lavatory." In one hand she held a clipboard at her waist, and in the other hand she swung a whistle around like a weapon. I immediately felt about Coach Heidi the same way I had felt about Mrs. D'Angelo ever since she had scolded me at the age of eight for throwing mud on Debby's little brother's Big Wheel: I was completely intimated by her, and my fear manifested itself by causing the back of my left elbow to itch relentlessly.

"And there will be NO visits to Big Bear after lights out," Coach Heidi bellowed across the dining hall, her voice the only audible sound in a room full of hushed ten-, eleven-, twelve-, and thirteen-year-old girls. That is, until I heard Debby's voice whisper in my ear.

"Yeah, right," she said with a laugh. "Coach H. clearly doesn't know the appeal of a talented Boy Scout."

I looked at Debby and silently shushed her, glaring at her with as much seriousness as I could, so she would know I wasn't kidding. But instead of heeding my warning, she looked amused. I had known Debby since the second grade when we had moved into her neighborhood. It was the first house my family had ever owned, and my mom was always bragging about the numbers: *three* bedrooms, *two-and-a-half* baths, *two-*car garage, *one-quarter* of an acre. But Debby had lived in a house all her life, and she was definitely more experienced than I was—both with living in a house and spending time with boys. She even appeared more physically advanced, though her own small breasts were really not much bigger than my tiny lumps. It was the way Debby held herself that made her seem older: she was tall, and she had perfect posture. She held her full head of thick, chestnut-colored hair high when she walked, unashamed of the summer freckles adorning her face like measles, and letting the light sparkle off her generous brown eyes in bronze-colored glints. She was the kind of girl who always got the Rizzo part when we acted out *Grease*, and I can still picture her strutting across the middle of our family room, singing "Sandra Dee" with all the lustiness she could muster from her thirteen-year-old body.

Standing next to someone like that always made me feel short, even though at five-foot-two, I was tall for my age and only a little smaller than Debby. But I had hazel eyes that never seemed to capture anyone's attention and straight, blonde hair that hung limply around my shoulders. It was so blonde that it almost appeared white, a shockingly bright color that sometimes startled me when I looked in the mirror. I knew nothing I had could compete with Debby. And over the years, she had told me stories I couldn't believe and showed me things I'd never heard mention of inside the protected walls of I.C.S., not the least of which was the story about the guy's hand in her pants, a recent triumph that had taken place two weeks before during a trip to Seaside Heights.

For me, Debby was, and always had been, dangerous. But that didn't keep us from being friends, from getting together most days after school and almost every day all summer. Even though Debby laughed when I told her about the things us I.C.S. kids did for fun and even though she called us prudes, I knew she liked me a lot. It didn't matter if I hadn't seen half the things she had—that was one of the reasons we got along.

I knew instinctively that she loved to tell me her stories, to watch my eyes reveal surprise at her latest stunt. And I loved to hear her talk, to imagine being Debby—going out with boys and letting them touch me wherever they wanted.

But it didn't occur to me until that moment that I had never really been in Debby's world. Until then, we'd been causing trouble all over our neighborhood—humping Ken and Barbie dolls in Debby's basement until Barbie's leg snapped out of it's socket, sneaking tampons out of her mother's bathroom even before we had a use for them, wandering for hours through the woods with boys we barely knew, taking swigs out of bottles we got from some of the older kids in the neighborhood—but we'd never actually left that world together, at least not without our parents. And as I looked at Debby that afternoon, still grinning and nodding at me the same way I'd seen her do a thousand times before, like the times when she would take a cigarette out of her mouth and hold it out to me even though she knew I wouldn't accept, I suddenly realized what I had gotten myself into. Involuntarily, I began to scratch the underside of my arm nervously and wonder what would happen next.

All of the Hidden Valley materials had warned about how cold the mountain air became at night. Though it seemed impossible to me in the middle of a sweltering July, I was extremely grateful when the evening set in that first night to be able to immerse myself in my down-lined sleeping bag. Debby had one too—hers was called "The Mummy" because it narrowed as it went down to her feet just like a Mummy's casket. It was the latest model, and I knew she had saved up for it all year.

That night in the cabin, Debby unrolled our sleeping bags on the two metal cots closest to the canvas wall on the east side of the tent. According to Debby, those two cots were prime real estate because they would be the first to warm up from the sun in the morning. Nobody questioned her when she did it, and I wasn't about to challenge Debby's knowledge and experience.

"Feet to feet," Debby said to me when I started to put my pillow at the end next to her cot. "That's the safest way to do it. Head to head, and you could get lice."

"What about head to feet?"

"Nobody does it that way." And she was right. Nobody did do it that way. But not long after lights out, two girls in our cabin named Becky and Amber did get up. They tiptoed out the door by Debby's head. I could hear their feet sliding through the already damp grass and their stifled giggles rising above the silence as they got a few feet away from the tent.

A flicker caught my eye: Debby's flashlight.

"Amateurs," she said, but I couldn't see her face so I didn't know if she thought it was funny or pathetic. "Going out the first night is like asking to get caught." The handful of other girls in the cabin murmured their agreement, and Debby clicked the flashlight off. As far as we knew, Becky and Amber never came back.

We didn't hear much else after that—except for the crickets and the night settling in around us. It was the kind of quiet I had never heard before: a natural silence, the complete opposite of the traffic noise outside our old apartment and even different than the steady buzz of the street lamps in front of our new house on Debby's street. This silence was pure, and though I expected the completeness of it to frighten me, it didn't. Instead I allowed myself to get comfortable with my awe, as if mesmerized by the soundless music.

H idden Valley didn't advertise its wake-up call in its full-color brochure. We had to be at the dining hall by six in the morning for breakfast, and when the smell of overcooked eggs and burnt-up little sausage coins reached my nose that first morning, my body lurched like I was going to upchuck. Debby told me to blow out through my mouth to keep the smell from coming in, and surprisingly her idea worked. The feeling dissipated. Coach Heidi had expressed her distaste for waste so I spent every morning after that hiding the revolting food in my milk, the Hidden Valley version of a diet shake.

Lunch and dinner were an improvement over breakfast but still not very appetizing. Nevertheless, as it was the only place to get away from the unrelenting Pennsylvania heat and humidity, my favorite place at Hidden Valley quickly became the dining hall. I had learned at our first camp-wide that every tribe (we were the Shawnee tribe, which was made up of the six cabins in our section of the woods) had to take turns being hoppers, the campers who helped prepare the hall for each meal. This meant setting the tables, preparing the condiments, filling the water and milk glasses and doing whatever else was needed. Though most of the girls hated being a hopper, I eventually sought out the opportunity. After two endlessly long days of staring with envy through the dining hall's plate glass window, watching other girls be hoppers, I found out that if I volunteered, I too could help inside where it was cool. Debby called me a kiss-up, but I happily left her in the sweltering heat and went in to help whenever I could.

At that first breakfast, I found out that Becky and Amber had been caught by Coach Heidi and put to work washing dishes—just as Debby had predicted and Coach H. announced after the morning prayers. As we delivered our used trays to the conveyer belt, I saw the two girls sweating among the piled-up dishes. Behind the steam that emerged from the gaping dish dryer, the stacks of empty white plates looked as if they could be porcelain skyscrapers floating among the clouds on a hot summer afternoon. Both of the girls looked exhausted— their soaking wet pajama sleeves were pushed up, and their faces were flushed with the pink hue of perspiration. I couldn't believe that Coach Heidi had kept them there all night, but there seemed to be no other explanation. It gave a girl pause, and for the first time since we'd started planning our trip, I wondered if I would have the courage to sneak out with Debby when the time came.

A s it turned out, it was a question I didn't have to answer for much longer than I expected. The next few days were spent suffering through our tiresome daily routine. Because of some cruel twist of camp fate, we swam in the mornings when the air was still chilly and hiked in the afternoons when the air was thick with moisture and mosquitoes. Each morning as we stood along the murky shore of Valley Lake—though the brochure had promised "acres of sandy beaches"—and waited to enter the not quite tepid water, the cold air whipped through us like tiny tornadoes, covering our legs with a rash of goose bumps and causing our nipples to harden.

Debby took one look at me the first morning and said I looked like a pile of zits. "Are you going to make it?" she asked, and I nodded without speaking, knowing that I had to keep up with her in and out of the water if I wanted her respect.

Coach Heidi stood on the long pier wrapped comfortably in her morning sweatsuit and blew the whistle every three minutes to signal the beginning of a new heat of swimmers. We swam laps for a full two hours that morning and every morning after that, fighting the choppy water until it was time to pull ourselves out of the lake, waterlogged, and walk the half-mile back up the hill to our cabins.

"I think I'm going to die!" Debby announced when we flopped down on our cots, and I didn't even bother to agree with her, so shocked was I by her admission of weakness.

After swimming, we were allowed a short forty-five minute break—"quiet time" as they called it—which was designated for writing home to our parents and keeping our cabins clean. Like everyone else, I did neither. Instead, we changed out of our wet bathing suits and back into our pajamas and lay on top of our makeshift beds, catching our breath and waiting for the next whistle to blow. Even Debby kept to herself, blinking off into sleep like the rest of us.

Afternoons were no less merciless. If you paid extra, you could go horse-back riding (which I thought sounded exciting and not all that strenuous), but for everyone else—me and Debby included—there were plenty of other laborious things for us to do. We alternated between playing some intense softball or kickball games (neither of which I cared for) and going for "leisurely" five-mile hikes up and down the foothills of the mountain that sat next to our camp. The entire time I was there, I felt as if, at any moment, I might simply collapse. And one afternoon, I even used the red scratches on my arms to fake sun poisoning and earn myself a solid hour of air-conditioned rest in the nurse's luxuriously cool infirmary.

During all this time, I kept waiting and waiting for Debby to make her move. Although I had not decided whether or not I would go with her, I was still anxious for the moment to come. I desperately wanted something dramatic, something unplanned, to happen; after all that was the reason I had come to camp in the first place—to experience something new, to sit around the campfire and watch the firelight dance in the eyes of my new Blue Bear boyfriend.

As it had turned out, we finally got together with the Boy Scouts for a rigorous softball game on Day Four. The only problem was that a Hidden Valley-versus-Big Bear softball game didn't exactly allow for much boy-girl interaction since we were sitting on one side of the diamond and the Boy Scouts were on the other. Still, it gave us ample opportunity to check them out, and Debby and I had started compiling a list of their assets before the first pitch had even been thrown.

"That one," Debby said, settling her gaze on a dark-haired Boy Scout with thick eyebrows and high cheekbones, "is as sweet as a popsicle."

He certainly was attractive and, more importantly, matched half of the young celebrities I had pasted on my walls: Scott Baio, Rick Springfield, Erik Estrada.

"But next to him—ewww!"

I glanced at the boy sitting beside him on the bench—who, oddly, had a mustache as thick as the one my gym teacher wore even though all of us campers were under fourteen—and had to agree with Debby. "What about the one on the other side?" I asked, nodding at a smaller, freckle-faced boy with silky hair hanging down to his shoulders. Shaun Cassidy crossed with Peter Brady.

Debby smiled. "Mary, you're hot for his bod, aren't you?"

I could feel myself blushing a little but glanced at the field to make it look like it was no big deal.

The Girl Scouts batted first, but neither Debby or I got a turn at the plate before the inning was over. We had both been assigned to the outfield—she was center, and I was left—so we spent the bottom of the inning waiting for a whole lot of nothing to happen. One Boy Scout hit a pop-up over first base, but Debby didn't even move when the ball arced in the right fielder's direction. I was relieved I had avoided being sent to right field since I hated that position. Catcher was my spot of choice, but I was almost never selected for anything in the infield.

It wasn't until the top of the third that Debby and I got a chance to bat, and by then, the Girl Scouts were ahead by one. Debby had worn her cut-off jean shorts and a nearly see-through t-shirt she tied in a knot above her stomach. When she sauntered up to bat in that get-up, swinging her tiny, newly teenage butt like it had a bell on it, everyone sitting around the field turned to watch. I'm sure they all believed that anyone as nubile and alluring as Debby would strike out, ending the inning, but I knew Debby would not disappoint, and she didn't, wailing on the first decent pitch like a natural, sending it to left center field, where two Boy Scouts stood there watching Debby shoot for first while it landed between them. The first baseman glanced at Debby with surprise, and she offered him a wink that said something akin to "There's more where that came from, fella."

Though I had no desire to follow Debby's pitch perfect performance, I was up next. I was keenly aware of the fact that every eye on the field was on me. As Debby's sidekick, I had them wondering if I too would surprise them.

But before I even got to the plate, one of the outfielders yelled in my direction. "What a shrimp," he said. It was the one with the mustache, and when I caught his eye, I held it and glared at him, a warning not to write me off. Back in the sixth grade at I.C.S., I had been one of the tallest kids in our class, but here on the Hidden Valley field—with the oldest campers, twelve to fourteen, making up both teams—I was a bit on the small side. And I certainly didn't have the muscles that some of the Boy Scouts were sporting in their homemade cut-off shirts. So I wasn't surprised when Mustache Man turned around and motioned to his teammates. "Move it in, boys. This one's going to be easy."

My dad had taught me to hit a baseball before I could add and subtract, and I knew that if I got the right pitch, I could send it soaring fast and hard into the outfield. But if I hit it too high, it'd be an easy pop-up, and if I hit it too low, the tallest of the Boy Scouts could reach up and grab it without leaving the ground. There weren't many shorties on the field, the smallest player behind me in the catcher's position and the rest of the boys who hadn't yet had their growth spurt lining the bench like limp noodles, including Peter Brady-Cassidy.

I glanced at Debby, who had one foot on first base and the other on the field, her legs making a perfect Isosceles triangle. She stood with her right hip jutting out into the field, and her hands were at her waist. I knew she was waiting to see what I would do—send her home or back to the bench, ending the inning—but I told myself I didn't care what happened, that Debby was on her own and had to prove her mettle all by herself. I was in it for me.

I took two balls before I got a good one, and that third ball went straight into foul territory, right over Peter Brady-Cassidy's seat on the bench. The next pitch came so quickly I hadn't even gotten my bat all the way up before it crossed the plate and a strike was called. So I had the bat up again before the pitcher could get another one by me.

I thought back to all of the company picnics and pick-up games my dad had taken me to, parading me out to home plate like a trophy. The guys on the other team always laughed—"This little girl, Jimbo? All right, whatever you say"—and then they'd throw me a soft lob, which I'd nail and hit over the shortstop's head, so it would land behind him and in front of the left fielder, running like hell for first base and sometimes second, all the while hearing my dad cheering to beat the band in my wake: "All right, Mary! Go, girl! You got it." I told myself then that my dad was just behind the dugout, clapping for me again—"You got it, Mary," he said—and when the ball flew towards me, I stopped thinking and let go, nailing it like I always did, only this time it flew over the left-fielder's head too because he'd come in so close, and I was past first base before I realized Debby was rounding third, her long legs gliding like a gazelle, easily making it home before the ball reached the plate. I stopped on second, hesitated, and decided to hold my spot. After all, the girls were up by two, and we had barely gotten started.

That night at dinner, Debby and I were stars, having helped the Girl Scouts destroy the Boys in a eight-to-three rout. All the older girls and the counselors were buzzing around us with high fives and pats on the back while we ate hot dogs and mac-n-cheese, easily the best meal we'd had since we'd arrived. But as dinner came to an end, the euphoria of the game wore off, and I found myself feeling deflated. Four days at camp, and I still hadn't even been within arm's length of a Scout unless I counted standing next to one on base, which I most certainly did not. It didn't seem right. I had come to camp for butterflies, but all I'd gotten was goose-bumped skin and sweaty armpits. So when we were brushing our teeth in the latrine that night, I got on Debby's case about it, even though I'd been asking myself a dozen times since Day One if I even had the guts to go out and risk getting caught by Coach Heidi.

"I thought you said we were going to get some action," I said to Debby in an uncustomarily in-your-face way.

"I believe I said *I* was going to get some," she said without looking away from her own reflection in the mirror. "You're on your own, Virgin Mary." It was a nickname I hadn't heard in months and one Debby had given me when we'd first met two years before. I'd been wearing my plaid school uniform, and Debby said it looked like a bad sofa pattern. I had thought the same thing every time I looked in the mirror since first grade and immediately liked Debby for both her astuteness and her lack of restraint. It didn't hurt either that I had the exact opposite impression of Debby. She was coolness defined: feathered hair, feathered earrings, and the Holy Grail of adolescents—Gloria Vanderbilt jeans. From that moment on, I saw her as perfection.

But while watching Debby admire herself that afternoon in the mirror of the camp latrine, I noticed a small boil that had formed on the left side of her nose. The freckles surrounding the bump had kept me from locating it before. I wanted to feel sorry for Debby, but she was so content with her own image that sympathy felt pointless.

"Well, why don't we go tonight?"

"Can't," she said simply. "It's only Night Four. I'm not going to risk the wrath of Hungry Heidi."

"We only have two nights left—what are you waiting for?"

"Night Five." Debby whispered the words "Night Five" as if they held some secret meaning, as if they were the most titillating words she would ever mutter, and she lifted her dark eyebrows at me as she spoke to emphasize her point. It was the same reverence with which she had spoken about Seaside Heights earlier that summer and junior high before that.

"What's so special about Night Five anyway?" After spending five days and four nights with Debby in the crappiest excuse for a summer camp I could ever imagine, I was getting tired of her attitude. I was beginning to lose faith.

"You'll see," she said and pivoted dramatically towards the door.

I decided to give her one last chance.

Night Five was the night of the big pajama party at Hidden Valley. Coach H. went on and on about how it was the last night us girls could be alone before the big dance on Night Six—which I reminded myself was Friday in the outside world, just one day before my release and before I finally got to go home—so everybody was supposed to dress up in their pajamas and sit around acting girly. But all I could think was that eating popcorn and making girl talk in my pajamas was the last thing I had ever hoped to do at stupid summer camp. As if I didn't get enough of that at home.

But before the humiliation of the all-girl pajama party, I had another hurdle to overcome. I had volunteered to be a hopper again that night, and unfortunately, two things conspired against my desire for an easy dinner: first, Debby decided to join me, and then Coach Heidi sat at my table. The reason Debby had decided to hop that night was completely different than my own and particularly underhanded. She had volunteered because it was spaghetti night—an odd choice given the ninety-degree heat—but Debby had an idea. She had some friends in the Ming tribe—girls who had been in Shawnee with her the previous year and who were the designated hoppers for Night Five. The plan was to steal one of the camp's huge bags of white cake mix and use it in place of the parmesan cheese that was supposed to be served in little bowls on the table with the spaghetti. In my mind, the plan would never work, and it seemed like a waste of time and energy in a place where you were left with so little of it. How did Debby hope to get in the kitchen? How could anyone get anything over on Coach Heidi? But while we were setting the tables, Debby came out of the kitchen wearing a shit-eating grin and carrying a huge silver bowl that was brimming with a pile of cream-colored dust. It was as if she carried gold.

She walked right over to me and said, "Try it."

I hesitated while she grew impatient.

"Before Heidi Ho gets here, okay?"

I licked my index finger and dipped it in the bowl, coating my fingertip with just enough to get a taste. When I put the finger in my mouth, the sweet flavor of Betty Crocker and birthdays floated on my tongue. She had done it.

Just then, the dining hall doors opened, and the campers started to flood in. As they waited in line for their spaghetti, Debby and the Ming tribe filled the fake wooden bowls that sat on each table with mounds and mounds of yellow cake mix.

I didn't want to do it. I knew we were asking for it, but there was no time to protest. So instead of worrying in my normal Mary way, I let myself enjoy the rebellion. I even reveled in it. I filled the bowls as high as I could, just like the other hoppers were doing. I skipped from table to table, happy to finally have revenge on the institution that had lured me from home with images of a teenage paradise it had failed to deliver.

But when I got my spaghetti and went to sit down, I saw that Coach Heidi had chosen my table to dine at that night. Instantly, I knew she would blame me. After all, I was the hopper, I had been in charge of prepping our table. Maybe she would suspect me of being behind the whole thing—hadn't I volunteered to help so many nights before? Coach Heidi always expected the worst of us, and I could imagine her accusing me, of questioning what other reason I could have had besides mischief for volunteering so many times. As I approached the table with my dented plastic tray and plate of watery spaghetti, I considered turning around and running as fast as I could away from the dining hall and Coach Heidi and the whole Hidden Valley fiasco. Or maybe I could just stand there and hope nobody saw me, maybe I could make myself turn invisible just as easily as I had once made it snow. In reality, though, I knew my only chance was to pretend I knew nothing, to act like everything was normal, to play the part of the innocent I wished I still were.

Instinctively, I reached for the cake mix. I figured my best bet was to pile as much of it on as possible. Coach Heidi had already sprinkled some on top of her plate, but when she saw me heaping it on, she reached for even more. I watched with fear as she dumped enough yellow cake mix onto her food to almost completely obliterate the red spaghetti sauce from view. I took in a deep breath and prepared myself for what could only be a disaster.

The camp chaplain stood and led us in the dinner prayer,

an unfortunately shorter version of grace than I had been hoping for, and then—the one thing I had been wishing could somehow be avoided—she invited us to eat.

I knew I couldn't hesitate, that to do so would only lead to my indictment, so I picked up my cheap camp fork and, with a bit of unexpected fervor, took a huge bite of my cake-mix-covered spaghetti. Just as I tasted the sugary vanilla crumbs swirling together in my mouth with the acidic tomato sauce, someone from a few tables away started coughing. It sounded like a choking animal, and without thinking I looked over to where the hacking girl sat. As soon as I settled my eyes on her gasping mouth, vomit shot out of it. I was sure that the sight of this combined with the repulsive taste in my own mouth would also cause me to throw up, but I stayed surprisingly calm and gulped the mouthful of noodles down just as cries of disgust and protest erupted around the room.

Luckily Coach Heidi had put the fork to her mouth and quickly put it down again when the commotion started. She hadn't tasted the concoction, and I knew this small miracle would be in everyone's favor. I looked over at Debby who, playing the saint, had run over to the girl who'd puked and started patting her on the back as if she wanted to help her. Her face showed no sign of guilt—she looked as innocent and pained as the mother of Jesus at the foot of the cross. I was surprised by how convincing she seemed, but I had to admit to myself that I had suspected all along she was going to get away with it.

For some reason, Coach Heidi never accused any of us hoppers—or any of the other campers either—of causing the small catastrophe. Looking back, it seems likely she was probably more concerned about someone pointing the finger at her for running a sloppy kitchen or maybe she was just anxious to get on to her favorite event of the week: the pajama party.

As soon as we got back to our cabin, Debby and I darted to the latrine, the only place we knew we could be alone. The instant we closed the door, we gave into our hilarity, exploding in fits of laughter that spewed out of our mouths like uncontrollable bubbles. I was hysterical. We both were. It was the only time I remember feeling that way with Debby— like we were equals, like we had done something together rather than apart. The effect was one I couldn't ever remember feeling before: it was euphoric. We went on and on this way, clutching our hands to our faces, both ashamed and proud of our clever deceit, until the last of our joy had finally dribbled out and merged with the soap scum on the sticky washroom floor.

After our coup in the dining hall, Debby was feeling especially generous. She told everyone who didn't know—including me—just what the annual pajama party was really about. She explained that Coach Heidi was a raving lesbian and that Hidden Valley was just an excuse for Coach H. to surround herself with fresh, young girls who were at the height of puberty. She talked about how the star softball players—the husky ones who'd slid into home plate on their chests and won the game for us against Blue Bear—were actually girls who played on Coach Heidi's softball team in Lancaster during the school year. She even claimed to have heard that Hidden Valley was just a cover for recruiting young lesbians. But Debby said she'd never bought that part of the story, that she'd been coming to Hidden Valley for five years and no one had ever laid a hand on her. She said she figured it was just a place for Heidi and her crew to hang out in the summer and harmlessly appreciate the young female campers.

Debby went on to explain that was why Night Five, the night of the pajama party, was the one night you could go out without fear of getting caught. Rumor had it that after Coach Heidi and her team watched hundreds of young Girl Scout campers parade around the dining hall in their best PJs and nightgowns, they were all so horny that they went off together and had a big lesbo orgy and that was why you never had to worry about getting caught sneaking out on Night Five.

"So Night Five is the only night of the whole week you can go out?" I asked, interrupting Debby for the first time. "What about after the dance?"

"The dance is a joke," Debby said matter-of-factly, completely oblivious to how much of my bubble she had burst. "It's cookies and punch. Besides Heidi's on red alert the night before we're supposed to leave. She figures we'll risk it then, if ever. And she's right—every year, dozens of girls get caught. Anyway, because I know what the pajama party is all about, I always bring my sexiest nightie, as a kind of thank you to old Heidi of the Hills." As she said this, Debby pulled a shorter-than-short pink cotton nightie out of her backpack.

"You'll freeze," one of the other girls said.

"I have my robe, and besides, it's worth it to keep Mother Heidi on my good side."

When the other girls had gone back to getting ready, I turned to Debby and said, "Do you really believe that? I mean about the orgy—it sounds so made up."

"I'm banking on it," Debby said as she pulled out her flashlight and made a show of sliding it into the pocket of her robe.

Then Debby turned to look at me, her voice changing from show-off Debby to real Debby. "Are you coming with me?" She asked this question in a tone that said she already suspected I wouldn't. But our coup in the dining hall had fortified me. If Debby could sneak out, so could I. And, besides, wasn't this the reason I had come to camp in the first place? Wasn't this what I had been fantasizing about as long as I'd been old enough to read?

"Oh, I'm coming," I said with the kind of certainty I usually reserved for doing fractions and diagramming sentences, and Debby gave me a appreciative smile that told me she finally saw me as her equal.

We left the pajama party early, sneaking out the back kitchen door while the prize for the camper who best epitomized the Girl Scout spirit was being announced, an award neither Debbie and I would receive and an appropriate coda to an evening of board games and girly superficiality.

Debby said we should hike up to the edge of the trees rather than walk through the open field that connected Hidden Valley to Big Bear in order to avoid detection. During the daytime, the woods at the top of the hill provided a welcome reprieve from the unrelenting sun, but at night, they were altogether different: a living, breathing organism where unknown wildlife lurked and serial killers hid from view. Every time I had to go to the bathroom at night, I felt as if I'd walked onto the set of a slasher flick, and I'd rush from our cabin to the latrine and back with only a flashlight to protect me, certain that night would be my last.

I had the same feeling on Night Five, the feeling that unavoidable danger waited for us inside the woods, but almost as soon as we crossed its threshold, my fears disappeared. The only noise was the sound of the trees sighing in the breeze, the only animals a couple of squirrels chasing each other like newlyweds. And once we'd traveled a few hundred feet in the dark, I realized there was probably nothing to fear. It hit me then that we were the ones to fear, we were the ones who were breaking the rules, passing through the forest like a couple of criminals, and that sense of conspiracy titillated me to no end. As we walked, I let myself imagine what we would find on the other side of the woods: a gigantic fire blazing in the night? A gaggle of drunken Boy Scouts howling at the moon? Or something even better?

But when we emerged from the dark trees, what we found was nothing like I had imagined. There were a row of cabins— real log cabins, not glorified tents—in a small clearing at the edge of the woods, and absolutely nothing else—no campers, no bonfire, no empty beer cans, no wet bathing suits, not even a stray fishing pole. The only thing that stood out was a single cabin, which was lit up like a department store, every window blasting incandescent light. It was so bright, in fact, that I could even see the moisture on the individual blades of grass.

"That's it," Debby said, nodding in the direction of the glowing cabin.

"How do you know?"

"I just know."

And, of course, she was right. When we got closer to the cabin, we could hear the sounds of "Owner of a Lonely Heart" wafting through the cold air like a siren. Debby never slowed her pace, walking right up the front steps of the cabin and knocking on the door as if she were an invited guest. The door opened almost immediately, and a Boy Scout who looked as if he was only standing because the door was propping him up waved us inside.

It was soon clear that the only reason the area outside the cabin was so immaculate was because absolutely every piece of trash the Boy Scouts could have accumulated during the past week was being kept inside—there were empty cans and wrappers strewn across the floor, stacks of magazines and tapes on every surface, and dirty towels and underwear in every corner. It was like the teenage version of *Sanford & Son*. To my horror, I even saw a used condom lying next to the overflowing trash can. Not to mention, the floors were incredibly sticky, causing the bottom of my Dr. Scholl's to resist my movements every time I tried to take a step.

As soon as I adjusted to my surroundings, I saw that all of the Scouts from our softball game were there—even Peter Brady-Cassidy and the Mustache Man. It was as if we had all been reunited for a re-match, only this time it was clear we were outnumbered, and they were going to win.

I hadn't noticed him at first, but as we moved farther into the room, the Scouts studying us like fine art, I finally saw that the boy Debby had been admiring was there too. He was sitting on a bottom bunk in a corner of the cabin, his feet flat on the floor and a can of Old Milwaukee in his right hand. I thought he had seemed cute at the game that afternoon, but up close it was clear that he was more than cute. He was beautiful: his olive skin was flawless, and his rich, chocolate hair was thick and full. Even the bare bulbs hanging from the cabin ceiling looked fiery in his dark eyes.

Debby slid down the wall until she was standing in front of him and then announced herself. "Hi, I'm Debby," she said.

"Ford," he said simply without rising from his bunk, and I wondered if I could ever trust anyone who was named after a car, who only gave one-word answers, and who looked so movie-star handsome.

"We're from New Jersey," Debby said, shaking her hair back away from her face like she was in a shampoo commercial. She was still wearing the nightie from the pajama party, but at least she'd hidden most of it with her slightly more modest robe. Still, the robe was loosely tied, and a sliver of Debby's untanned skin was visible beneath the pink cotton.

"Me too," Ford said.

"What part?" Debby asked.

"Cherry Hill."

It was obvious that Ford wasn't interested in conversation, but Debby did not give up.

"I've never been there. What's it like?"

"Boring," Ford said with a snort.

"Same as Bridgewater," Debby added. "That's where we live."

But this time Ford did not respond. He had turned to look at the Scout sitting on the bunk next to his.

"Crash, what the hell are you doing?" Ford asked the other boy, who was flipping through magazines at a frenetic pace.

"I want to take that picture of Farrah with me," Crash said.

"Relax, you've got almost a whole day to find it."

Debby laughed at Ford's comment, an obvious attempt to catch his attention, but he still didn't look back in her direction, instead lifting his beer can to his mouth and taking a long swig. After that, he lay back on his bunk, and we could no longer see anything but his bare feet. There was no excuse for his disappearance, no "excuse me" or "goodbye," and I felt an immediate desire to flee.

Before Debby could make her next move, Mustache Man showed up with two unopened cans of beers in one hand and an open one in the other. "You girls want a cold one?" he asked, and Debby said yes while I studied the wiry hairs underneath his nose. It didn't look entirely different than pubic hair, and when I realized this, I felt a mixture of the jelly beans and popcorn from the pajama party rising in my throat. I lurched past him before he could put the can in my hand and made it to the door where I stuck my head out to catch my breath. When I had finally regained control, I shut the door and turned back around to re-trace my steps, only to find that by then Debby was sitting in Mustache Man's lap, laughing at something he had done or said, I couldn't be sure which.

"Is that your friend?" someone said, and I looked over my shoulder and saw that the voice belonged to Peter Brady-Cassidy, his long hair falling in his face so much that I almost couldn't make out the soft green color of his eyes.

"Kind of," I said, embarrassed by Debby's behavior. Was she really going to hook up with Mustache Man? Couldn't she see how gross he was?

"She's out of control," Peter said.

"Yeah, I'm getting that feeling."

"I'm Jeremy," Peter said, and he offered his hand to me like we were adults.

"Nice to meet you, Jeremy," I said because it seemed like the kind of thing you said when someone offered you their hand. "I'm Mary, but nobody every calls me that besides my parents."

"What do they call you?" Peter asked.

The only thing that came to my mind was Virgin Mary or Mary Measles or just Measles, which is what the kids in my school had been calling me since I was the first one to get the Chicken Pox in second grade, but obviously I couldn't tell Peter Brady-Cassidy to call me that. "I don't know," I said. "Just M., I guess."

"Okay, M."

I wasn't sure what to say next, so I looked back at Debby for help, thinking that just seeing her face would give me some brilliant idea about how to continue the conversation. But instead of finding inspiration, I came across a picture of her sucking face with Mustache Man, her tongue darting in and out of his mouth, dangerously close to his revolting mustache.

"Oh, God," I said and reached for the door again, this time going all the way through it and out into the cool night.

For some reason, Peter followed me.

When I'd gotten a safe distance from the cabin, I stopped and turned to look at him. His hair had fallen back in his eyes, but I could still make out the freckles on his tanned skin.

"That was totally disgusting," he said.

"No kidding."

"I hate girls like that."

"Like what?" I asked him.

"Girls who—"

But before he could finish, the door flew open, and Debby came running down the steps. "Mary," she yelled. "Mary, are you out here?"

"I'm over here," I said without yelling but still loud enough that I knew she could hear me.

Peter stepped over to the line of trees, as if he instinctively knew that Debby and I needed to talk alone.

"Mary, what's going on? Are you leaving or what?"

When we'd been in the latrine, hours earlier, I'd thought I'd go along with everything Debby did that night. I thought I'd drink cheap beer until I puked and grope a boy I didn't even like. I'd thought the feeling I'd had after the cake mix incident—the high of doing something daring for a change and actually getting away with it—was what Debby always had and I always wanted. But when I thought more about it and remembered the look on her face, a look of true wonder, a look that said, *I can't believe what just happened*, it told me that she hadn't felt that way before either. That she didn't feel it any more often than I did. That it wasn't something you could plan or manipulate. And I knew if I followed Debby's lead that night, I might have some fun and I'd definitely have a good story to tell back at I.C.S., but I also knew that wasn't what I really wanted and that I'd rather go back to the cold cabin all by myself, that much closer to going home, than do something just to impress her. "No," I said. "I think I'm going to head back and freeze my butt off in the cabin instead."

Debby took a deep breath, and I wondered if she would try to convince me to stay. Instead she looked at me and said, "You can use the Mummy if you want."

I took this as Debby's way of saying she was sorry if I didn't get what I'd wanted on the trip. I decided the best thing to do was accept her apology and move on. "Thanks," I said, and before I could read the look on her face, she turned around and ran back to the cabin, back to the arms of Mustache Man.

"So you're leaving?" Peter Brady-Cassidy said out of nowhere, causing me to let out a little scream.

"Oh my God," I said. "I forgot you were there."

"Sorry about that."

I looked in his green eyes—he'd pushed his hair behind his ears—and saw that they were as beautiful as any girl's. "Yeah, I guess I am," I said, answering the question that still hovered in the air between us.

"I get it," he said.

"You do?" I asked him.

"Yeah, sure," he said. "You don't want to be like her."

I let out a little laugh, surprised that he knew exactly what

I'd been thinking. And even though I'd never done it before, I knew that if we were going to kiss, this was the time to do it, that I could lean towards him right then, and it would happen. Like magic. I looked up at the sky and saw that all the stars were out—Cassiopeia, the Big and Little Dippers, Orion, even Venus was visible at the bottom of the horizon.

"Goodbye, Peter," I said as I started to walk away.

"Mary," he said before I had taken more than two steps away from him.

I turned back to him and saw his hair glinting in the glow of the cabin.

"It's Jeremy," he said.

"I know," I said with a smile and turned again, this time walking into the woods without looking back.

At the cabin, I didn't go right to sleep, but I didn't stay up wondering what Debby was doing either. Instead I allowed myself to enjoy the haunting silence of the evening, the one thing I had come to appreciate from my time at Hidden Valley.

When Debby came back just after four that morning and woke me so she could share all the sordid details of her one night out, I wasn't really interested in hearing about it. I played along, smiling and acting surprised at all the right moments, but it just wasn't the same. I couldn't believe that after all we'd been through in the past week—the crappy food, the nights below freezing, the sweltering days, the makeshift "cabin," the toxic latrine, the unsanitary communal showers, the near-torturous amount of exercise, not to mention the money our parents had dished out—after all that, Debby thought this, four or five fleeting and insignificant hours she had spent groping some hairy Pennsylvania hillbilly who probably did have lice, was actually worth it. Such a revelation was a disappointment to me as authentic and disorienting as when I first found out that Santa didn't exist or that death is unavoidable. It was the first time I was completely let down by someone I really cared for.

As I sat there listening to her detail each and every last kiss, each and every touch, I wondered what it was that Debby really wanted and what it was that drove her to a place like Hidden Valley year after year. It couldn't simply be the promise of one night of some seriously heavy petting, could it? There had to be some other reason why she was happy to leave her regular life behind. There had to be something else that was missing.

And so I tried to remember what Debby had acted like when we'd said goodbye to our parents nearly a week before, what emotions had been betrayed on her face, but no matter how hard I thought about it, I just kept drawing a blank. All I could picture were my own parents: my mom in her wrap-around dress, my dad in his Rutgers t-shirt. The two of them waving and clapping as if I had just hit another unexpected home run.

Pictures of the Day I Was Born: A True Story

Part of me wishes I could go back.

Back to the time before I met my birth mother.

I found her during my thirtieth year, figuring we'd exchange letters for a while, maybe even talk on the phone if we felt brave enough. But before I fully understood what was happening, she was on a plane headed for Ohio, where I was in my first year of graduate school.

Barbara came bearing gifts—a t-shirt advertising the family business and a gold necklace adorned with a claddagh heart. Immediately I wondered if I would ever wear it. Because, unfortunately, I don't wear gold. Just silver. But how could I tell her that?

After Barbara left, the first thing I did was call my mom.

My real mom.

That's what I call her when I have to distinguish. There's my real mom, and then there's Barbara, my birth mom. But usually I just call her Barbara.

"I can see everything for what it is now," I said to my real mom on the phone that night.

"Really?" she said. "What does *that* mean?"

"It means that I was worried I would feel conflicted. That I wouldn't know who my real family is. I used to feel guilty about it, but it's not the same anymore. Now I know you and Barbara are two different parts of my life, and that's all right."

But as soon as I hung up with Mom, the guilt returned.

I felt like a traitor, betraying my mom and dad, the people who had raised me, the people who'd stood by me my whole life. I wanted to call my mother back and tell her I would never talk to Barbara again. I wanted to tell my mother I loved her, that she was the only mom I needed. I didn't realize how transparent I was being until my husband asked me what was wrong. I could feel him circling, searching me for clues, but I didn't want to give in to his interrogation so soon.

"What did your mother say?" he finally asked.

"You know what she said. The same thing she always says."

"Let me guess. She *said* she was fine with Barbara being here, but you don't believe her?"

I didn't respond. I didn't have to.

Dave knew he was right. He knew my family as well as I did, and he'd heard our story over and over.

My younger sister and I were both adopted before we were six weeks old. Like kittens. Just old enough to be weaned, but not old enough to remember. Except we're not from the same litter.

In 1970, I was born in Baltimore, the illegitimate daughter of a student nurse whose ex-boyfriend had returned from Vietnam not long before I was conceived and said he wasn't ready to start a family when Barbara missed her period. After she let me go, I spent just over a month in a Catholic orphanage before meeting the two people I would come to know as my parents, the two people who would love me unconditionally for the rest of my life.

My sister Katie has also met her birth mother, but her story is still more of a mystery: her mother Marie was only seventeen when Katie was born in 1973, and her upper-middle class parents pressured Marie into giving Katie up for adoption. On Katie's eighteenth birthday, as soon as it was legal to do so, Marie filed the paperwork to find out what had happened to her baby. Not long after that, she received the information in the mail and called our home just to make sure her long-lost daughter was safe. But to this day Marie has never revealed who Katie's biological father is.

My parents never hid the fact that we were adopted. Before I was old enough to read, I was able to recite by memory the story of how I came to be their daughter. And they always said they would support us if we wanted to look for our birth mothers or any other family.

They said it, but I never believed it was true.

I believed, instead, that doing so would be uncomfortable for all of us. That it would hurt our special bond. So I never thought about it in any serious way. It simply wasn't an option. I was at least *that* devoted to my parents—devoted enough that I wouldn't consider the one thing I was afraid would truly wound us.

"So what are you going to do?" Dave eventually asked me after I had gotten off the phone with my mother, my *real* mother, and realized I *should* do something.

"I don't know," I said. "Maybe I'll email her. It's too late to call back." It occurred to me then that email was actually the best option. It would give me the chance to go over some of the details we didn't get to on the phone, and it would allow me to do so without having to deal with any more of my mother's endless questions.

Dear Mom and Dad,

I just want to let the two of you know that everything went great with Barbara this weekend. Besides feeling a little like I wanted to throw up while I waited for her flight to come in at the airport, it was smooth sailing. I really can't believe how easy it was.

Yes, she looks a heck of a lot like me, and we have much in common. Barbara talks as much as I do, she's just as open as I am about everything (she's totally fine with the adoption and how everything has gone—it's amazing how well-adjusted she seems), and she also tends to lose track of time and run late like I do.

On the other hand, it looks like I got my desire to plan everything in advance from Mom. Barbara was content to wing it, but I kept hearing a little voice in my head saying, "What are we going to do next?" Dave and Barbara practically had to tie me to the sofa.

Well, I guess that's all for now. Hope you are doing well. I'll talk to you more soon.

Molly

I considered signing the email "Love, Molly." I desperately wanted my parents to know how much they meant to me, how much I loved them, especially since one of my worst fears was that they would read Barbara's visit as an attempt to replace them. But since I'd never signed my messages that way before, I also worried they'd find it unusual. Would they think I was acting strange? Or worse yet, would they see it as an attempt to alleviate my guilt? And that was when I realized that's exactly what it would have been.

The truth was that I have never been the kind of person who signs messages with the word "love" or relies on predictable sentiments to express my feelings. In that way, I am more like my dad, keeping my most important emotions to myself, so ultimately I opted to leave it out, instead trying to simply be myself, which until that moment had always seemed easy.

Barbara married my biological father, Dan, one year after she gave me up. The wedding took place six months before their second child Danny was born. Dave likes to joke that the two of them had yet to figure out where babies came from. After Danny, Barbara and Dan had three more children: Ben, David, and Terri. So we're all fully related. Not half brothers and sisters, but the real thing.

The adoption agency found Barbara eight months before her visit, mere weeks after I had filled out the necessary forms and passed the required psychological tests. It was during one of those interviews when the issue of my birth father first came up. I was told to prepare for the possibility that Barbara might have reunited with him. These things happen, they said. So I was aware of the possibility, even if it made me rather anxious.

But when we found out for sure, the shock hit my husband Dave hard, as if he never really understood the whole thing was actually happening. Suddenly, I had more family than he did. Overnight—or thirty years later depending on how you looked at it—I had inherited an entire brood.

I met Dave during our junior year in college. We lived on the same floor in the dorm but didn't hold a legitimate conversation until I was wandering around Read Hall looking for strangers to photograph for my photojournalism class. We had only been introduced a few hours earlier—Dave's grip firm enough to impress me when he shook my hand—so when I spotted him across the lobby, I figured he would still qualify as someone I didn't really know. At the time, he was sitting at a table with his friend Dexter, who I'd soon learn was one of the most direct people I'd ever meet.

Dexter's interrogation started immediately. "What do you want to take our picture for?" he asked.

"It's for class. I'm supposed to take portraits of strangers."

"But you met me three hours ago," Dave pointed out.

"I won't tell if you won't."

I shot an entire roll of film while we talked, careful not to let Dexter know that three-quarters of the photos were of Dave. As I worked, I told them about the class: "My professor claims some students meet the person they'll end up marrying while shooting this assignment. As soon as he said that, all I could think about was how something like that would *never* happen to me."

"For all you know," Dexter said, "you two could end up

married some day." He looked at Dave and then at me, connecting us with an imaginary line.

I blushed and stood up, moving away from the table where the two of them sat.

"I think I have plenty," I said, holding up my camera as an explanation.

"Don't let him intimidate you," Dave said. "He's just compensating for his own insecurities."

Dexter was skeptical. "As if," he said simply, but I still felt a sense of relief pass over me. I had always wanted to find someone like Dave—someone who wasn't afraid to say what was really on his mind—but I never thought I actually would. The strange thing was that, even that first day, Dave sensed that about me. He tuned into my apprehensions as readily as most guys tune into a football game.

"Don't talk to any more strangers," Dave advised before I left. "They say it's dangerous."

Sometimes I think Dave has always known me, sometimes he even knows what I want before I do. Like with Barbara. Dave wanted to know where I came from before I could put words, or even thoughts, around my yearning.

"But aren't you curious?" Dave asked me when I first told him I was adopted.

"Not really." We were eating dessert when the subject came up. I swirled my spoon around the chocolate chip ice cream melting in the bowl in front of me while I considered his question. I really wasn't curious about my biological mother, but I also wasn't ready to admit any more than that so I said,

"I guess I never thought about it."

"You *never* thought about it?"

I tried to explain. "I have a great relationship with my mother. We talk about everything. I don't ever lie to her. It's not always easy, but it works. I don't need another mother."

Dave leaned back in his chair. He was just barely nodding his head, as if taking in my words, trying to find some new angle. Finally, he went on. "But what if you're an heir to some throne? What if you're a Kennedy?" He paused before continuing. "Don't you want to know?"

Dave would speculate this way for hours, but I knew his interest was deeper than just wanting to know if I was related to royalty. Slowly, carefully, his interest in my past became my desire to find Barbara. But at first the inclination was his. Before Dave, the birth mother question was the one I was always afraid to ask.

B arbara looked like me, stood like me, and talked like me, but even after she had come and gone that first time, I felt as if she were as odd and unknown to me as any stranger we could have picked up at the airport that day. And for all of our similarities, she was nothing like I had imagined she would be.

When she got off the plane she was wearing a lavender-colored twin-set with dark violet flowers embroidered on the surface. Her hair was shorter and less kinky than mine, but it was exactly the same shade of brown: the drab color of day-old tea. I did not inherit her muddy brown eyes, but I feared that the deep lines crawling across her skin like flesh-toned spiders would some day be mine. As soon as I saw her,

I knew instinctively I'd look just like she did some day.

Back at the airport on Sunday morning for her flight home, she protested as she took her glasses off for one last snapshot: "You'll see my wrinkles."

I pretended I didn't know what she was talking about. We stood under the artificial lights of the terminal, smiling, an arm around each other like old friends.

Driving back from the airport, Dave told me it was strange to see someone who resembled me so much. I knew his words meant more than he was willing to admit. I was pretty sure Dave wasn't completely comfortable with the idea of Barbara once she was a real person and not just an imaginary character we invented as we lay in bed trying to fall asleep. Maybe it was because Barbara and I are so physically similar. In one picture from that first visit, we look like a perfect match. Just like one of Barbara's sweater sets. Maybe Dave was afraid that knowing Barbara would make me more like her. I'd start getting wrinkles and wearing mom jeans.

And yet, I couldn't help but wonder if all of the guilt and anxiety I was feeling at that time was Dave's fault. Maybe, if it hadn't been for him, I never would have looked for Barbara.

Maybe I would never have wondered who I really am.

When I was a kid, I didn't think about it much—being adopted. My parents told me it meant I was special. They told me that only someone who loved her child more than herself could give her up, and I believed them. I still do. And when I was little, I told other kids that *I* was special, that *my* parents had paid for me.

But when they cleaned out their basement a few summers ago, my parents found the receipt from my adoption, and I discovered exactly how much special costs.

Two hundred dollars.

That was the amount on the Catholic Charities sliding scale appropriate for a young Navy couple who couldn't get pregnant.

All kids fantasize about having different parents at one time or another, but adopted kids have the license to take it a step further, identifying celebrities who they imagine look like their genetic match. When I was nine years old, I watched the *Dukes of Hazzard* and daydreamed about John Schneider being my long-lost dad. Then as a teenager, I started to believe it was Art Garfunkel. In college, I had settled on Bob Dylan as the most likely possibility. The only requirements seemed to be that he have curly hair and be famous.

I never fantasized about having a birth mother. In fact, just the idea of such a person made me uncomfortable. And by the time I started daydreaming about my unknown father to "Bridge Over Troubled Water," I was smart enough to know I fantasized about birth fathers because my own father was too busy with work to spend as much time with me as I would have liked. Sure, I knew he did this to make certain we never went without, but that didn't make me miss him any less.

Like many kids in my generation, I saw my father in pieces while I was growing up—at dinner if he wasn't out of town and on weekends, though sometimes that meant going to the office with him. Most of our other activities revolved around the things he liked to do: we would jog, fish, or play basketball; we would go to the library; and we would visit the dog pound. The pound was the only one of those places I actually longed to visit, and dogs—especially down-and-out, needy ones—were an interest my father and I shared. So, on Saturdays, after a particularly grueling run, we would reward ourselves with a trip to the city-operated animal shelter that sat adjacent to the high school track.

The cement-block building that housed the pound was as dirty and pathetic as you would expect. The stale smell of urine and the super-potent toxicity of industrial cleanser worked in conjunction with the high-pitched howls of the abandoned dogs to give me a headache that would often take hours to shake. As I walked along the cages, I tried not to think about the idea of numbered days, and, for the most part, it never bothered me. I was so happy to be with my dad and so eager to adopt a pet that I could look past the small imperfections during our time together.

Sometimes we would take one of the dogs on a walk. It was on such occasions that I would give in to my emotions and end up in tears, begging to take the animal home as my father led me quickly back to the shelter to return the miserable little pup.

Despite my many pleas, we never did get a dog from the pound. My mother was worried about poorly trained or rabid dogs, and she didn't care for mutts. She wanted a purebred, and eventually that was what we got.

After Barbara's visit, I thought about the dog pound and couldn't help but wonder why we went there so often if we were never going to take anything home. I would have asked my parents for an explanation, but I knew exactly how they would respond. My father wouldn't have much to say, and my mother would say I think too much. She'd tell me that my father took me to the dog pound because I liked it—simple as that—and that I should worry about more important things like my thesis. I'd eventually interrupt her with more questions, and finally she'd retaliate by telling me I push people too much, attacking me where she knew it hurt most.

My whole life my family has accused me of overthinking things, of interrogating them without reason, and it has always been a sensitive subject, especially since they were the ones who taught me that good relationships were based on communication. But too often what they really wanted was for me to reveal my innermost thoughts and feelings without requiring the same of them. Rather than admit this, they routinely accused me of pushing them to their limit.

"You never give people a chance to finish, Molly," my mother said to me on the phone mere hours after we'd dropped Barbara off at the airport. "You are *always* one step ahead of people, finishing their sentences for them and going on to a new thought."

"I didn't do that with Barbara," I said. "I'm not like that with everyone. Just you. You're family."

"Well, aren't we lucky?"

I knew my mom was kidding, but I also knew she would

have preferred to get a pass—like the one I'd given Barbara for the time being—every now and then.

Dear Molly,

Your dad says hello, and we are both happy for you. You are at a perfect age and maturity to handle meeting Barbara now, and I am glad it has worked out for both of you.

We already know from what you have told us about Barbara's letters that she has many qualities and talents that you have inherited. She has an ability to feel comfortable around people. She is thoughtful and creative.

Molly, I am really glad Dave is with you for support. This is an important time in your life. Relax and enjoy it. It will be over sooner than you want it to be. And, yes, there will be many questions that you forget to ask. A lifetime cannot be reviewed in a week end. Enjoy Barbara and cherish her and her family. I hope her flight home was a good one.

With lots and lots of love,
Mom & Dad

On the phone that night, I told my mom that meeting Barbara made me realize I was too hard on them, but all I could think when I read Mom's email message was that "weekend" is one word, not two.

Both my sister and I wanted to take piano lessons when we were young, but, like most parents, Mom and Dad were hesitant about such a big investment. We had a four-bedroom Colonial with a landscaped yard and an in-ground swimming pool, my dad was a vice president of a division of a Fortune 500 company, and we vacationed at the Jersey Shore, but for some reason we still couldn't buy a used piano.

After much persistence, Katie and I finally convinced my parents to let the two of us enroll in piano lessons on a trial basis. For six weeks, we trudged a block up our suburban street to practice what we learned on a piano at a neighbor's house. When the trial period was over, my mother kept promising to work on my father about getting a piano, but nothing ever came of it. Except that I can still do scales. And because of all the money they saved, we all get to vacation at their condo in Florida, which even I can admit ended up being worth it.

Barbara turned out to be the opposite way with money. She told us during her visit that she gave my biological brother Danny enough money to buy a car and that, at the age of twenty-four, one of my other biological brothers was still living at home.

After college, my parents had high expectations for my sister and me. They wanted each of us to get a place of our own and claimed that people who supported their adult children did them a disservice, citing a distant cousin who'd lived off his parents his whole life as proof. As it turned out, their tough-love approach worked—both my sister and I have been independent since graduation, never having to call their bluff.

Money is not the only thing that's different between our families. I was a stellar student, but Barbara's kids—my four brothers and sisters—have all been diagnosed with learning disabilities, problems that have to do with things like hyperactivity and not being able to pay attention. I wonder sometimes how I escaped.

Or if I really did.

My mother's words come back to me over and over again: *You are always one step ahead of people.* What does it mean to have such a gift? At times my brain feels like it's on speed, racing ahead of me at an unwise rate of travel. Maybe thinking fast is more of a liability than an asset.

In school, I was always in the gifted and talented classes. I suppose that means I did well on tests and refused to believe it when people said I couldn't do something. And when I failed a class my first year of college, I never felt like a failure, never even contemplated such a possibility. Instead I did as little as I had to do to get an A the next semester. Although I was educated enough to know that bad grades didn't mean I was dumb, I'm not sure they tell that to kids with learning disabilities, and I can't help but wonder how my life might have been different had I grown up in Ellicot City, Maryland, with Barbara and Dan.

When I found out that Barbara and her kids were all jocks, I was at a loss. Katie had always been the athletic one in our family. But the only two people in my entire biological family to attend college went on athletic scholarships. I still can't figure out how that makes sense given everything they say about DNA and the nature-versus-nurture debate or even, more simply, what it means about me.

"Do you like country music?" Barbara asked me on the second day of her visit.

"Not really," I said and regretted it at once. I wondered if I was I supposed to lie about such things.

"Oh," she said, and then she paused. I'm not good at pauses. I like to fill them up with words. Everyone knows this about me. Well, everyone who knows me knows that, and I realized then that Barbara didn't really know me at all. I feared I had hurt her feelings irreparably because I don't like songs that twang. I let myself imagine that our relationship would end before it ever really got started. But then she spoke again: "I was just wondering because we have karaoke."

I looked at her, not sure what she was talking about. The word "karaoke" tapped on my brain like a knock-knock joke.

"At the restaurant," she added, as if she knew I was confused.

I had forgotten about the restaurant. *Their* restaurant. The family business. I told myself to pay better attention. Barbara's husband Dan, my birth father, and his mother ran the place. Even though it's called Daniel's Restaurant, food is an afterthought, and it mainly appeals to bikers because—thanks to an unusual grandfather clause—they can pull their motorcycles up to the outdoor bar and have a beer without moving too far from the leather seats of their bikes. Everyone in the family puts in time at the restaurant: the kids all have regular shifts, Barbara's sister works on weekends, and Barbara pitches in for big events.

Much to my surprise, I also found out that Barbara had

been employed for over thirty years by the hospital where I was born. Like a criminal returning to the scene of the crime, she worked in the maternity ward, helping deliver the babies of others.

"We have it on Tuesdays and Thursdays, and we all get up and sing." Barbara was still talking about the restaurant, but I was having trouble focusing.

Knock, knock. Who's there? Your mom. Your mom who? Your mom who sings karaoke.

"Do you sing?" she asked.

"No, I can't sing at all," I said. "Never could." My next thought was that it was strange that the person who had given birth to me was able to sing well enough to perform in front of a crowded bar. And with that realization came another: maybe Barbara wasn't really my biological mother after all, maybe there had been some mistake. But before I had time to fully consider that option, I looked at her face and saw the truth: no one had ever looked like me before, and Barbara could have been my twin. I wasn't sure whether I should have been relieved or disappointed.

"Are you a good singer?" I asked her.

"God, no!" She blushed as she spoke and chuckled a little to herself. "I'm a horrible singer. But I don't care. I just get up there and do it. We all do."

Later she showed me pictures of the karaoke-singing family from Maryland. She told me they all get up and sing "Family Tradition."

Together.

I hoped my distaste didn't show on my face.

After she was gone, Dave cracked up and said I'd almost surely have to join them when we visited. I didn't laugh with him because I couldn't fathom how I would get out of it.

B efore we met, Barbara and I talked on the phone. She sounded different long-distance than she did in person. I didn't have the face, the body, to go with the voice. All I could go on was what I heard. I had photos, but they weren't a living, breathing being, so it was her voice that gave me a moving picture. I saw a teenager, young and awkward, nervously tripping over her words. But that picture was wrong. She was the opposite of that—sure of who she was and comfortable with it. Solid. A delicate rock.

As we ate breakfast during her visit, I listened to her words echoing in the air in front of me and recalled my original picture of Barbara. Her voice sounded gravelly because she had just woken up. Mine does the same thing in the morning. I was surprised again at how many of our different pieces seemed to match. Every hour of her visit I noticed something new, and I wondered if other people noticed those things all their lives.

hey molly,

i just wanted to say hi real quick before i run off to class. my mom (your mom too!) is flying to see you today. i am sure you are aware of that. don't be too nervous. there is absolutely nothing to worry about. i am going on a road trip to charleston, south carolina to see my boyfriend, romas. i am very excited. he said that it is in the upper eighties there so i am taking my bathing suit. have fun with my mom and take care of her. i am sure you two will love the time you spend together. i will talk to you when i get back. good luck.

love,

terri

My biological sister Terri always writes "love, terri" at the end of her email messages. She only found out that I existed eight months before Barbara's visit, but she has loved me online ever since. I don't even say those words to my real sister, Katie, or my parents. I tried to ignore it at first, hoping she wouldn't do it again. But she did. *Every time.* Finally, I gave in. Now I sign my messages to her the same way. I feel as if I must.

I bought birthday cards for Barbara to take back to my biological brothers Ben and David. I reluctantly signed their cards, "Love, Molly." It was two months after we started dating before I put such a declaration in writing to my husband, and yet I found myself doing so with two strangers. I worried that, like me, they would find the salutation overly effusive, that they wouldn't know Terri had started it, that it was just a family thing.

Then I asked myself—they are family, right?

Terri called twice during Barbara's visit. The two of us had talked on the phone before, but that weekend her voice—like her mother's but younger, more boyish—sounded strangely unfamiliar. So when I heard her on the other end of the line, I passed the phone away quickly, as if it were diseased.

Despite my contact with Terri, I avoided Danny, Ben, and David—my three biological brothers—completely those first few months. I'd never had any brothers, and I didn't know how to do it. I felt sure there was some trick, some secret brother language I had yet to learn.

And they were nothing like Dave or my father, so my relationships with other men didn't really help either. In the pictures Barbara sent me, they wore wool ski hats and plaid flannel shirts, thick, dark whiskers covering the pale skin of their jaws. They looked like they could beat somebody up. They looked like they just had.

When I first saw the pictures, I was shocked. I expected to see six people who looked exactly like me. They were my flesh and blood after all. But when I saw six faces with different bone structures and different eyebrows than mine, all I could think was, why didn't they look more familiar?

Now I know what to look for: Terri's smile, Ben's nose, Danny's forehead. And even though I look exactly like Barbara did at my age, it took me a while to see even that—as if I were blind to my own likeness. I had initially expected to see a mirror image, but I finally figured out it's all the pieces together that make the picture whole.

After Terri called, Barbara tried to figure out if Terri was ovulating.

"I don't think Terri and Romas are sleeping together yet," Barbara said. "At least I hope they're not."

I was silent. I thought maybe Barbara would know what that meant. But she didn't know me well enough to read my signals. She didn't know I only kept my mouth shut when I didn't want the wrong words to come out—I knew Terri and her boyfriend were sleeping together, and I knew Terri was on the pill. She had said as much in her email messages.

"We get pregnant easy in this family," Barbara added with a laugh.

"Really?" I said as I imagined myself with a basketball under my t-shirt.

"I got pregnant with Danny while I was on the pill."

When I told my mother about Danny's conception, she said, "You have *got* to tell Terri."

"Why?" I asked.

"She could get pregnant. She has to use a condom." My mother's plea sounded rather frantic, and I wondered why she was so invested in Terri's ability to procreate.

"I don't think that's the kind of thing I can email her, Mom," I said, trying to imagine how that would go.

Dear Terri,

I know this is going to sound strange but your mom told me today that she got pregnant with Danny while she was on the pill so I told my mom, and she said you should use a condom even though you're on the pill.

Hope you are having fun in South Carolina with Romas!

Love,

Molly

Right around the time I started looking like a woman, my father began treating me differently. I had a huge growth spurt when I hit puberty, and by my thirteenth birthday, I looked more like a co-ed than a kid.

I clearly remember when my father first took notice of how much I had changed. It was the night of my eighth-grade graduation, and I was wearing one of my mother's old dresses. The knee-length skirt was shimmery and blue, and it followed my curves just closely enough to draw attention to them. My father watched me walk in the room, a surprised look on his face, and then told me I looked all grown up. For weeks, I wore his approval like a precious jewel, but after that, it seemed like we started to grow apart.

Dave always says he imagines the hardest time for a father would be when his daughter begins to take the shape of a woman, that he too wouldn't know how to relate to a child who is developing breasts and becoming desirable to other men. I understand what he is saying—I even believe it—but I still wish it had been easier for us to stay close during that time.

Dan, Barbara's husband, gave her a red rose wrapped in plastic to pass along to me during her stay. Immediately I suspected that it came from a gas station they passed on the way to the airport. I've never liked red roses, but I tried to appreciate the thought. Unlike Barbara, Dan hadn't written me, and he hadn't called. It was almost as if, to him, I still didn't exist.

When I talked to my mom after Barbara left, she was quick

to bring up the one part of the visit I didn't want to talk about: "Did Barbara ask if you were mad at Dan?"

I was angry with Dan—still am—but I didn't want to admit it to my mother. I was angry with him for breaking up with Barbara when she got pregnant with me. It felt like he'd abandoned her. Like he'd abandoned us. But I knew that my anger had never really been about simple rage. It was about fear and apprehension.

Barbara told me that the night before her visit, Dan said he wasn't sure if he was comfortable with her coming to see me. And she responded by saying he didn't have much choice in the matter.

I was surprised he hadn't mentioned his hesitation until the night before she left. When I asked Barbara about it, she said Dan wasn't very good at being open with his feelings.

Then I remembered something Terri had said in her first email message. She'd admitted she didn't think her dad would know what to say if he ever met me. Remembering that made me feel even more edgy and uncomfortable about the whole situation than I had before—the same way most people feel when getting a shot.

"I'm not mad at him anymore," I said in answer to my mother's question, knowing I'd already told her that at least twice. "I forgave him the second Barbara told me he felt bad. There's no use being angry with someone who knows he screwed up. He feels lousy enough."

"All right," my mother said, but I wasn't sure if she was hearing me, which made me want to change the subject.

"You'll never guess what Barbara's first car was," I said.

She paused to think, and then in an energetic voice began to say the name of her first car: "A Karmann—" She stopped before she had completed her words.

"Yes, a Karmann Ghia!" I said, forcing myself not to wonder why she had hesitated mid-sentence. "Isn't that weird?" I was determined to smooth over my anxieties. "You both had the same car."

"We did?" she asked, disbelief in her voice.

"I guess that's something else you shared," I said.

My mother was silent on the other end of the line, making me wonder what had caused her to stop talking, what she was thinking. Suddenly it occurred to me that I had inadvertently compared her to Barbara, something I had never wanted to do to either of them. And then the guilt came back to me all over again. And, for a second time that night, I found myself wishing Barbara's visit had never happened.

My mom has a lifetime of memories with me. Good memories and bad memories, exhilaration and exasperation. More than forty years of me, for better or worse.

The only thing Barbara has that my mom doesn't is the day I was born. And obviously I don't remember that. Barbara took pictures though.

Pictures of the day I was born.

I'm quite a bit smaller than I am in any of the five-week-old baby pictures my parents have. I have hardly any baby fat yet, and my skin is the color of bubble gum. As I studied the yellowed images of the first day of my life, it occurred to me that it was odd there weren't any pictures of Barbara, but only pictures of me by myself.

"Why aren't you in any of the pictures?" I finally asked.

Barbara's head jerked up. She looked directly at me without speaking, her eyes bigger than I'd ever seen them before.

I knew instinctively that there was something she was trying not to say. Like me, Barbara only stopped speaking when it was too hard to get the words out. And then it hit me: she wasn't in any of the pictures because she had been alone. The day she had given birth to her first child, Barbara had been all by herself. No one to take her picture. No one to hold her hand.

"You weren't supposed to take pictures," Barbara finally said. "But I didn't know that until I'd already done it. I couldn't believe how much you looked like me. None of the others looked that much like me." And finally she dropped her eyes back to the snapshot, running her finger delicately along the white border.

Yes, she had that one day my mom didn't. But I knew then Barbara would have happily traded it for all of the others.

Barbara left a card behind. Snuck it into our bedroom when I wasn't looking. Dave was in on the plan.

I opened it after I emailed my parents. My name was written on the envelope, and there was a little flower drawn next to the scripted letters. The card had a picture of Monet's "Pond Lilies" on the front. I had already noticed how well Barbara picked out cards. They featured famous works of art or quoted well-known writers.

Dear Molly,

Every day I offer a silent prayer of thanks that such life was placed in my hands and that now I am being blessed with the miracle of touching even a part of it.

I felt that perhaps this early birthday gift would be a gentle reminder to you of how much I treasure the gift of your life and hopefully the friendship we will share.

Happy Birthday today and everyday.

Love,

Barbara

It was the gold necklace. I couldn't help but think, *if only it were silver.*

In the car on the way back to the airport, I had complained to Barbara about how my mother could never pick out gifts for me. "She doesn't understand what I like," I said, selling out my own mother for a quick moment of connection. But when I saw the gold necklace, I realized how wrong I'd been. Barbara didn't understand me any better than my mom. The cards were just a fluke.

I also noticed that Barbara used the word "blessed" the same way my grandmother does: "We are so blessed," Grandma always says. My real grandmother, that is.

On the other hand, Dan's mother—the only one of Barbara and Dan's parents who was still alive—didn't even know I existed. Barbara had admitted that when Dan broke up with her after she got pregnant with me, he never told his mom what had happened, and even when Barbara came to visit me, he still hadn't worked up the courage to tell his mother the truth. In her mind, that weekend was like any other—she thought her daughter-in-law was attending a nursing conference, not meeting the child Barbara and her son had given up thirty years before.

Dear Molly,

We've been thinking about you and did try to call you once. I hope all is going well for you and Dave. I know your birth mother is coming to visit soon. It will be an emotional experience, and I will be anxious to talk to you. But no matter what, you belong to us.

We love you very much. Have a great visit and a very special love to Dave too.

Grandma & Grandpa

P.S. Get something you'd like from us for your birthday.

My grandmother's words were the ones I couldn't get out of my head after Barbara left.

But no matter what, you belong to us.

She sounded so sure of herself. So proud. I had worried that Barbara's visit would cause doubts for everyone in my family, but my grandmother was unshaken. To someone who doesn't know her, my grandmother's assertion may have sounded possessive or proprietary. But I knew she said it only because she was confident about who she was and what family meant.

If only she could have cleared it up for me.

I didn't see either my mom or Barbara on my actual birthday that year. My parents were in Florida for the winter. They're retired and like to joke that they're spending my inheritance. My birthday was two weeks after Barbara left, but she told me I was born thirteen days late, no surprise since I clearly inherited my tardiness from Barbara. As we hurried down the airport corridor to her gate only fifteen minutes before takeoff, she joked about how she couldn't remember the last time she'd been to a flight so early.

Barbara made it safely back to Maryland that night. She called after I talked to my mother, saying I should fly out to see them soon. I reminded her I don't fly and, just like I do with my mom, said, "Remember?" before I could stop myself.

I couldn't sleep after talking to Barbara. Instead I lay in bed wondering about all the changes that had taken place that weekend. And when the digital clock on the bedside table changed from 2:59 to 3:00, I realized that Dan, my biological father, would just be driving home from closing the bar, reminding me again how different my life had been from theirs.

The gold necklace sat in a blue leather box next to the clock. I could see the outline of it in the dark. It reminded me of the rosary my grandmother bought me when she and my grandfather had made a post-retirement pilgrimage to the Vatican. The clear glass beads came in an ornate green-and-gold case that I carried with me everywhere, clutching it like a life jacket when I used to fly. They say the Miraculous Medal will protect you from fatal harm.

Over time, the metallic paint wore through, revealing a

dull gray fabric, but still I clung to it for safety. Then one time during takeoff I realized I had forgotten it. I closed my eyes and prepared for the end, but nothing happened.

After that I stopped going to church.

That night I wondered if the blue box would have the same fate. Since I knew I'd never wear the necklace, I'd carry it with me instead. Like a talisman, it would protect me. Or maybe it would help me finally understand.

Dear Molly & Dave,

Thank you for a wonderful week-end. It was all I expected and more. I feel like we've known each other for years. The two of you seem to share a special relationship. Continue to grow as the unique individuals you are, and I'm sure you will continue to grow in love as one. Be good to each other and love tenderly.

God bless,

Barbara

P.S.—the money is for all the phone calls.

Barbara's thank you arrived a week later. "Damn it," I said out loud when I saw the word weekend split in two. A twenty-dollar bill fell out of the envelope.

"What's that for?" Dave asked.

"Phone calls."

"How many phone calls did she make?"

"Not twenty dollars worth."

"It's our inheritance," he said.

"I blame you for this mess," I said, but I let out a half-smile. And then I thought about what that word meant, *inheritance,* and what I had gotten from my parents—a love that never waivered—and what Barbara had given me too—a life that could never be repaid.

It made me wonder if I would ever be a mother. And if so, what kinds of gifts would I leave behind for my children? What would *I* have to give them?

Then I imagined myself writing a letter to my unborn daughter on *her* thirtieth birthday. The letter would say something like, "Hope to see you this week-end. Love, Mom." And there would be a pair of silver earrings tucked inside the envelope. My daughter would let out a breath of disappointment at the sight of the sterling jewelry, thinking woefully about how she only wears gold.

Shopology

My name is Emily, and my mother is an addict.

A shopping addict, that is.

I don't mean to imply that Mother is addicted to buying things or spending money. She's not exactly what I would call materialistic. Rather she's hung up on walking the aisles and surveying the merchandise. She likes to take it all in, to carefully consider which blender packs more of a puree punch. For her, such comparisons are like a science: an involved study of the numbers and options associated with every product on the market.

Shopology.

Sometimes she disappears for hours. Lost time, we like to call it. She drops by the Fresh Foods for a gallon of milk and becomes so immersed in the world of dollars and discounts that time stops altogether. Even the singing cell phone in her Coach clutch can't stop a binge once it's started. Hours later, she stumbles in the door, apologetic but still disoriented. An unpacked grocery bag reveals dozens of overpriced indulgent foodstuffs, crack for shopping junkies, but, alas, no milk. Eventually, we determined she shouldn't be allowed to wander out on her own.

"I just have trouble making good choices," she says, defending her behavior like only an addict can.

Truth is, she doesn't have enough to do with her time: no hobbies, no interests, no job. She spends her time cruising the strip malls for entertainment because she has no occupation. A typical case, really. Except, of course, her lack of employment is the result of being retired.

When I visit, we set limits: fifteen minutes for groceries, thirty for shoes.

Nevertheless, she sometimes falls off the wagon.

Take last Thanksgiving, for example.

Around two in the afternoon, my mother decided that we needed more butter while presiding over the turkey. She claimed she'd be "back in a jiff" and was out the door before I could call for reinforcements, leaving me to worry over an oven full of casseroles and a bubbling pot of giblets. An hour and a half later, the bird was overcooked, and my mother still absent.

Once again, she had strayed.

My father called the neighbors, hoping she'd stopped off for a chat, but no one had seen her. My brother hit the usual suspects—the strip malls, the grocery, the big box stores—but her Volvo wasn't to be found. The three of us stood around the kitchen, picking at the turkey and eating spoonfuls of stuffing out of a nine-by-thirteen pan. Another hour passed, and the mood became tense, pessimistic. My father was on his third Manhattan, and my brother had lost interest. I suggested a call to the authorities, and Dad caved. In a big city, four hours wouldn't have warranted much of a response, but in a town small enough to make Pizza King a formal dining experience, a mother missing on Thanksgiving Day was like a fire at an elementary school. Everyone was concerned.

When the police finally located her—at the Shop-n-Save Mini-Mart on Highway Fifteen—they said she had a blank look on her face: her eyes as glassy as a holiday lush. She sat on the dirty floor with cans of nuts and boxes of crackers strewn around her like satellites.

"For the life of me, I just don't know what to serve before dinner," she tried to explain. "Cheese puffs or candied pecans. Or maybe a nice olive tapenade."

After that, she stopped cooking. Now we spend each and every holiday in the buffet line, the price fix a prison sentence for junkies like Mom.

Joy to the World

Dearest friends and family,

Seasons Greetings from our house to yours! As you can see from the enclosed photo, we have a new addition to our family. Over the summer, the two of us traveled to China for a conference called "Meltdown Schmeltdown: How Wal-Mart Can Save Small Publishers Suffering through the Economic Crisis."

During our time in the Red State, we adopted the cutest little puppy in the whole wide world—a pure bred named Mingmei. While we are disappointed that we were never able to have a puppy of our own, we are simply overjoyed about the addition of Mingmei to our family. From all indications, she received excellent care in the factory where she was made, and as long as we don't squeeze too hard, her stuffing will stay inside her fur-covered cavity.

Luckily, we were able to move into a new home this year. This was not an easy decision for us to make, but after much discussion and thoughtful reflection, we took the big leap and moved across the hall to a slightly roomier, five-hundred-square-foot apartment. While we will miss the humiliation of washing vegetables in the bathtub, we feel that the extra room is just what our growing family needs.

We both started our second year in the M.F.A. program at the University of Phoenix this past fall. Things have been going well at school, although there have been some setbacks. For instance, we had thought we were among the favorites of our department chair, but when we heard about him sexting another graduate student, we felt somewhat left behind. Oh well, we'll just have to work even harder to get ahead in 2011!

School has allowed us some wonderful opportunities to travel, however. In addition to our trip to China—where we stayed in a room we rented from a trio of sisters who were honestly the three noisiest women we have ever met!—Katelyn made the seven-mile trek to the library four times during the fall semester, and once in mid-October, Kip attended his office hours. Boy, were the students surprised when he walked in!

Kip did manage to publish some stories this year and even sold one for actual money to *Perez Hilton* over the summer. That paycheck means that he has now earned .0012 cents for every hour he has spent writing.

We also feel fortunate that our families have enjoyed good health this past year. Even the Swine Flu has an upside—we both lost those five nagging pounds just in time for the holidays!

As in years past, we will be having a traditional Christmas again this year—spending too much money, buying things no one needs, driving long distances, aggravating ourselves and each other—all while growing ever more removed from the original intent of the holiday. And we wish you and your family the same kind of happiness.

Have the merriest of Christmases and a wonderful new year!!!

> Much love,
> Kip, Katelyn, and Mingmei

The Other Man

"What is it that you see in Danny anyway?" you ask me over dessert at the most expensive restaurant in College Park. The one the professors go to when they entertain visiting writers, the one all the other grad students think is too pricey to bother with—which, of course, makes it all the more appealing to you even though your credit card bills already eat half of your graduate stipend. Despite your record debt, you insist we find out what all the fuss is about, and for some reason I can never say no to you.

Our waiter thinks we are a real couple; he doesn't notice the way you look at *him*. And I have to admit we look good— no, great—together: you in your charcoal gray Calvin Klein sweater, the one that sets off your olive skin so well, and me in my black halter dress and Jimmy Choo slingbacks. It almost feels like we *are* in a real relationship, and I even think we might make it through the evening without a disagreement until the subject of Danny comes up.

After taking a moment to consider your next step, you continue: "Is it his status as a college dropout, his employ as a techie geek, or his wake-and-bake habit that you find so appealing?" You stop talking to scoop up the rest of the tiramisu we are sharing.

Sure, Danny is all you say he is, but that's just the surface stuff. What I like about Danny is that he is different. Maybe it *is* his lack of education and his drug habit, or maybe it's his thoughtfulness and his strangely possessive cat. Bottom line: he isn't like other guys. How many guys keep cats that want to scratch their lovers' eyes out? And even when he is high—which I admit is mostly all the time—Danny's eyes look as clear and blue as the kind of ocean you only see in travel brochures. When I look at him I think of dinner cruises and parasailing and Margaritaville, and even though I know they shouldn't, these images give me a sense of contentedness, of peace. But these are all things I can never share with you. On the other hand, I *can* tell Danny, and I do. And we joke around about going to one of those all-inclusive resorts and lazing on the beach in our own private cabana.

It is Danny's ability to do this with me—his ability to dream, to laugh—that makes me feel like I am getting the real him, not the notion of whom he thinks he should be, the way it is with everyone else. I know you think it's time for me to move on. You've said as much. But I'm not interested in relocating when Danny feels so good.

"I guess he just seems real," I say, my words sounding more like a question than an answer.

You run your tongue across your upper lip, collecting the remaining sweetness, and give me a look I've seen too many times before. "But it's not *going* anywhere," you say as you dab your mouth with the cloth napkin, and I wonder why it is that you always talk about where *I'm* going rather than where *you* are right now. From the moment we met, you've been more interested in critiquing my choices than making your own. It was three years ago during an awkward graduate school orientation: me hovering by the snack table, afraid of saying the wrong thing, of sounding like a fraud; you confidently moving from group to group with your jargon-heavy insights and analyses. I swooned over your vocabulary, your swagger, and I longed for the way you seemed at ease with every author discussed. Within a week, I was following you around, hoping your understanding, your credibility would rub off. Your constant critique seemed a small price to pay for your attention.

But as long as we've known each other, I can't remember one time when we talked about *your* future. Sure, we talk in general terms—about what kind of guy you'd like to be with, about where you'd like to live after you finish school—but it is never about anything real or concrete because your whole life has become about abstract things: about the dissertation, about theory, about pedagogy. I can't even remember the last time you socialized with anyone besides me.

By all rights, you are my best friend, and I love you in *that* way, that gay-best-friend way, but sometimes I think you want me to live so you don't have to.

The first time Danny convinced me to try Ecstasy with him, he refused to have sex. He mumbled something about it being too much.

"Too much?" I said, seeking clarification.

"Yeah, you know? *Too* much."

I laughed and thought about how you always talk about Danny's inability to articulate. He's no Joyce, you like to joke.

You know I've never been one of those people who does a lot of drugs—that's one of the reasons we could hang out. We agree that life itself is a better high than anything artificial. But I never pretended to be totally clean either, and I like to get stoned as much as the next person. But it took weeks for Danny to talk me into E. I won't lie to you about it now, though I hid it from you before: as clichéd as I know you'll think it sounds, it was simply amazing, it was phenomenal, it was the best sex I ever had with my pants on.

When Danny lightly ran his hand along my arm, I felt it all the way down to my core. Of course, I couldn't tell you about it, with your codes and your ethics. But I secretly wished you could feel it too. And more than anything I wanted to tell you how much trust I felt for Danny once it was over.

After dinner that night, the tiramisu night, I lie on Danny's bed alone, thinking about your questions and tracing imaginary pictures on the ceiling. I know I should be thinking about where Danny and I are going, about how he always says he's not into the commitment thing, about how he never talks about who he dated before me, but instead I think of the way it felt the night he touched my arm, the goose bumps on my flesh. I know we don't make sense—he doesn't get Faulkner, and I don't understand code—but somehow we connect.

I don't notice Danny walk in the room until he speaks. "Are you thinking about *him* again?" he asks.

I roll away and put a pillow over my head so he won't see my face flush.

"The *other* man," he teases.

I laugh, and he pulls the pillow gently away. I look at his eyes and involuntarily think about snorkeling. He kisses me, and things progress as usual. Something about Danny makes me feel more comfortable being myself than I have ever felt before—as if there is nothing wrong with desiring sex or being naked, as if there are no rules. Things have never been better between us than they are that night, and for once, the cat lets us sleep in peace.

"But what do you talk about?" you ask over lunch a week later at a new pan-Asian place you found in the District. "You can't just fuck *all* the time." You pause and add, "Or *can* he?"

"Isn't this the best green curry you've ever had?" I say, trying to change the subject.

You put your chopsticks down pointedly, set your hands on the edge of the table and lean in, your eyes goggling me like a happy hour drunk. I know you're trying to be amusing, but I also know you won't let it go.

"I don't know what we talk about," I offer. "What does anybody talk about? What do *we* talk about besides food and who's sleeping with whom in the department."

"We talk about fucking literature, that's what we talk about!" Your voice rises just enough to make me uncomfortable, and I look over my shoulder to see if anyone is listening. You ignore me and go on. "We talk about film, for Christ's sake. We talk about the beauty of art, or have you forgotten?"

I want to believe you are right, that we only concern ourselves with such important matters, and a few years back, I would have bought it, but now, I know enough to understand this is mostly a pose. "Speaking of film, what are we seeing this weekend?"

"Why don't you see a movie with *him*?"

"We *can't* see a movie together, remember? All we do is fuck."

"Oh, yes, I forgot." You snort and become distracted with collecting noodles on your chopsticks. I know I will have to give you a real answer sooner or later, so I think about the conversations Danny and I have shared—the ones that didn't revolve around Club Med.

Some nights we climb out his apartment window and take the ladder up to the roof. We sit in rusty lawn chairs and try to find the stars behind the yellow haze of the city lights. Sometimes we talk, other times just look. All I know for sure is that it is there, on the tar roof of Danny's apartment, that I most like to wait for another night to pass.

"I don't know what we talk about," I say. "Sometimes we talk about what we want to be when we grow up, or how things are different than we imagined they would be."

"You mean, he talks about what he'll be when he grows up, and *you* say you'll wait for him."

"I'm not waiting for anything. I'm content with the status quo."

You snort again. "And by that, you mean the fucking?"

"Would you please shut up about that?" I look around the restaurant as obviously as I can, hoping you'll honor my request.

"I'll say one thing," you add. "He must be *fantastic* in bed."

That weekend Danny and I go to a movie or a film as he calls it. Danny says Hollywood movies are nothing more than product placement, and films are the things I see with you. Danny laughs a couple of times, and I can tell he likes it because his body is slumped to one side the way it does when he first slides into a comfortable high. I smile and loop my arm around his. It feels nice to have someone to touch in the dark of the theater for a change.

When the movie ends, I grip Danny's arm, so he can't get up. I don't want to have to tell you that he failed our test. We both always say a guy isn't worthy if he can't sit through the credits. That not doing so demonstrates a lack of introspection.

When we walk out, I ask Danny what he thought.

"I don't know," he says with a grin that tells me he's trying to hide something. "It was entertaining and all, but what was the point?"

I think about how you would answer such a question, then compose my words as carefully as I can. "The point," I say, "is to show that reality is a construct, that nothing is actually real." In my own mouth, your words sound forced; my old feeling of fraudulence returns.

"Yeah, right," he says and looks away from me as if he's irritated, as if he'd rather be somewhere else. It's a look I haven't seen on him before.

"Didn't you at least like the use of a nonlinear chronology?"

"Why can't they just let a story be a story?" he asks. "It was a good story, wasn't it?"

"Yes, it was," I concede.

"So why not let the story speak for itself?"

"It's an artistic choice," I say, thinking this should be obvious.

"Sure, it's artistic," Danny says. "But it's nothing new. It's only innovative if it's never been done before."

I can't think of a reason to argue.

"Let's get out of here," he says as we approach his car. "Or wait a second! If the car is just a construct, then I guess we're not going anywhere, are we?"

"Very funny," I say and wait for him to open my door.

That Monday at school I tell you about my excursion with Danny. You listen attentively as I describe my impression of the imagistic direction and tell you how the lead actor made me so hot I couldn't wait to get back to Danny's place.

"And what did Danny think?" you ask when I finally stop rambling.

"Danny thought the film lacked innovation because the director was just emulating techniques we've seen so many times before." I want to sound convincing, so I add, "He thought it was derivative."

"Is that what *he* said?"

"Who?"

"Danny?" you ask. "Did he actually *say* 'the film lacked innovation'? And does he even know what the word *derivative* means?"

I don't answer. Instead I look over my shoulder to see who is rustling down the hallway. "Hi, Kara," I say as one of our fellow grad students walks by the open door of your office. For a moment I imagine what would happen if she just kept walking, if she went down the stairs and outside, never to return again. It's a thought I have been considering a good deal lately. And when I turn back to your probing face, I am suddenly aware that I am growing tired of your questions.

When I speak again, it is in a whisper: "I don't want to talk about this anymore." I sense that I need to be as firm as possible, more explicit, if I am to avoid further interrogation, so I add, "I don't want to talk about Danny."

"I don't want to talk about him either," you say in a dismissive voice, as if I am one of your students. Your brusque manner surprises me. Even for you, it seems bitchier than usual. I sit back abruptly, and you go on before I can regain control of my emotions. "I don't think you should see him anymore. You might as well just end it."

I wonder if you are becoming the controlling and manipulative person everyone says you are. I think about what it is that makes you think you can tell me what to do. I say, "Just because you're in graduate school doesn't mean you're smart. Maybe you don't like him because he just *is* smart."

"No," you say matter-of-factly. "I don't like him because he's not veracious." You pause, as if waiting for me to consider your words. My mind goes directly to the place in my brain where I have hidden away my questions about whether or not I can trust Danny, the place where I put all the days I don't see him, the times he forgets to call. But I don't want to betray my insecurities so I quickly disguise my unanswered questions with a look that feigns disapproval. You continue: "I simply don't want to see you get hurt. I care about you, that's all." Your voice has taken on that paternal tone I despise so much, and I feel the need to get away from you before anything else is said.

I stand up, alerting you to my departure. I want to shove my empty chair at you, I want to injure you—not because of Danny or anything you've said—but because you and I don't make sense anymore.

Instead, I just leave.

As I drive away from campus that afternoon, I decide to go right to Danny's. He's working on a freelance job, debugging or something just as vexing. He takes the time to kiss me even though I have shown up unannounced. While he finishes, I lie on his bed and play mind games with the cat, teasing her with one of Danny's socks.

Later, Danny and I order chicken wings for dinner. We decide to eat on the roof, and when we finish, I loft the bones into the alley without a thought to littering or consequences or anything else: my small rebellion. Danny asks what's wrong, but I can't tell him the truth because the last thing I want is for him to hate you even though he's not that kind of guy. I can't lie either; you know I'm no good at that.

"Maybe we could talk about it later," I say.

Danny is good at taking hints, and he changes the subject, but that night things never feel right or easy like they usually do. And later, while Danny breathes deeply, I am unable to sustain sleep. I wake with a jerk, certain the cat is working her magic, putting a spell over Danny and me and our dreams.

You and I don't talk for days.

Three to be exact.

This is how we always fight, so I don't worry about this altercation being any worse than normal even though I wonder if it should be. The phone rings on Thursday, and I know it's you because of the time: ten minutes after two. You always call then, just after your last class. I pick up on the first ring, just happy you've made contact. But you sound distant, and I realize this time our wound hasn't healed on its own.

"Can you come over tomorrow night for dinner?" you ask.

"*You* are cooking?" I'm skeptical.

"Just come over and see." You barely say goodbye before hanging up.

I arrive at your house promptly at seven. I know you don't like it when people are late, and I want to put things right between us, so I'm catering to your way of doing things: being on time, wearing the pashmina you gave me for Christmas, and carrying a bottle of Beaujolais.

You open the door as if you see me coming—even though your window doesn't face the street. It isn't until I get to the doorway that I sense you are not alone.

"Am I early?" I ask, confused by your lackadaisical demeanor.

Your mouth is pursed into a sour knot. Instead of answering, you jerk your head back, indicating something behind you. You haven't been on a date in years—no one's ever good enough—so I can hardly believe what I think you're trying to say.

I cross the room in a rush, stopping at the door of your bedroom. At almost the same moment I see him, I realize what is happening: I know it is Danny who is there with you. Am I surprised to see him there? Not as much as you might think. I know you are trying to prove something to me—about his loyalty, about his sexuality, about who he really is.

Danny is asleep in your bed, his pale, hairless chest rising and falling with his breath. Even though his body is covered by the sheet, I can tell he's not wearing anything. It's a familiar sight, and if I try hard enough, I can almost pretend it's like any other day when I come out of the bathroom and find Danny asleep in his own apartment.

I walk over to the mattress, sitting gently on the edge. With just the tips of my fingers, I brush his shoulder. I know he won't respond; he's always been a deep sleeper. I can feel you watching me, wondering what I will do next, but I don't care about you anymore. I lift my legs to the surface of the bed and inch back into the curve of Danny's body, just as I've done before. Danny puts his arm on top of mine, and I close my eyes. It feels as close to home as anything does these days. As I lie inside Danny's shell and wait for him to wake, I start to imagine what will happen next.

The funny thing is that I know your attempt to break things down would only make us stronger if I let it. Now I can see the parts of Danny I couldn't before. I understand that I can't cage him in any better than you can control me.

And it's thinking about the word control that makes me finally understand what I have to do.

So, no, I won't ride off into the sunset with Danny, but I won't do it with you either. Maybe I'll leave the world of abstract thought and unread manuscripts behind for good. Maybe I'll opt for something more real, something more mundane. I'll book passage on a Carnival cruise line and go all out: play shuffleboard by day and drink mai tais through the night. I'll gorge myself on the all-you-can-eat buffet and make friends with other swinging singles. But, don't worry, I won't ever forget you.

I never could.

In fact, I'll be sure to send you a picture postcard—you know the kind with artificial-looking aquamarine waters and loopy cursive script. I know you'll be embarrassed when it arrives in your postal box, that you'll wonder who might have glimpsed your name above the address as you clutch the pastel-colored card against your well-toned chest. And just knowing that I've managed to put a tiny little scratch on the inscrutable image you project to the world will be more than enough for me.

Acknowledgments

First and foremost I need to thank Scott Douglass and Craig Renfroe for believing in my work and development as a writer. It is safe to say the two of you have changed my life.

Second, I would like to thank everyone who has generously given me feedback on my writing since I wrote my first story more than fifteen years ago: Jane Shore, Maxine Clair, Faye Moskowitz, Daniel Vilmure, Eric Goodman, Constance Pierce, Jim Reiss, Kay Sloan, Tim Melley, Buddy Nordan, Sandra Scofield, Josip Novakovich, Brock Clarke, Jim Schiff, Michael Griffith, Nicola Mason, Kelcey Parker, Suzanne Warren, Sarah Domet, Susan Carpenter, Terri Hammond, Brian Nealon, Andy Radcliffe, Mark Budman, Alex Taylor, Amanda and Ann Angel, and especially Lee Martin.

Also a special word of appreciation to Tracy Williams, Shelley Zimmerman, Jennie Vanderpool, Kara Thurmond, Rachel Tumidolsky Hardwick, Peggy Davis, Meredith Love, Kristin Czarnecki, Tasha Mehne, Sherry Hamby, Kristi Key, Jill Rausch, Tom Hunley, David LeNoir, Mary Ellen Miller, Dale Rigby, and Karen Schneider as well as all of my amazing colleagues at Western Kentucky University: your friendship means more to me than I can say.

It is incumbent on me to thank the Taft Foundation for their support of my work.

I would be remiss if I did not thank my family—my sister, Katie Brandt, and my parents, Mike and Penny McCaffrey—who have been nurturing my creativity and loving me unconditionally all of my life.

And finally to my husband, David Bell, who has never questioned my willingness to believe.